A Bomb in the Palace

BY JEROME G. SILBERT

A Bomb in the Palace

ISBN-10:
ISBN-13:

Library of Congress Control Number: TXu 2-168-368

Chapter One

Chicago, November 2016

It was 5:15 p.m. A time when a ringing phone at the law office was usually a wrong number. The staff had said their "good-nights" and "see ya tomorrow." The formality of the day fell away. Nightfall settled.

Joe Daniels loosened his tie and opened the bottom drawer of his desk. Like a trusted friend, his bottle of eighteen-year-old Macallan stood by. He waited an appropriate minute and reached behind for a glass. Fortification was the courage needed. Tonight, he would make his move. Damn the wife, the new beach house, the mortgage, he didn't want any of it. Not even the new BMW parked in his spot. Strike a blow for freedom. Strike a blow… He chuckled. "Yeah." He picked up the bottle and slowly untwisted the cork cap. His hand shook slightly as the rich liquid filled the glass. He took a long look at the perfect, deep sherry color. He raised the glass to his lips and let the scotch trickle into his mouth. Oh, the taste…the smoothness. The liquid was "*L'eau des dieux,*" the water of gods. He leaned back in his chair and half closed his eyes.

She was a new attorney at the firm. Her office was down the hall. She had a smile that seemed meant only for him. He had been through this before. Tits and ass were his thing. Monogamy was for the moment, if ever. But she…was different.

He opened his eyes and enjoyed another sip. The e-mail he'd sent that afternoon contained nothing incriminating. It was innocent, business-like. "Nicole, there's a new matter we need to discuss. Could you stay a bit after work?" He didn't have to say more. He knew she'd be waiting at her apartment. He congratulated himself on his subtlety. Experience is how life pays. He finished his drink, then deleted the e-mail from the computer and the server. *Can never be too careful.* He went into his private bathroom and freshened up. The image in the mirror was not bad for a man in his forties. His hair was dark and full. A hint of a five o'clock shadow on his face made him appear rugged, perhaps mysterious. Otherwise, he was in good shape with just the beginning of a middle-age paunch.

He grabbed his keys from the desk and put on his suit jacket. He went out the back way so that his departure wouldn't be noticed by security. *Can never be too careful.*

He was sure his wife, Beth, of fifteen years wouldn't question his lateness when he got home. It was nothing new. It had existed for most of their so-called marriage. He stifled his laugh. Her desire for him and his for her had plummeted like a bad day on the stock market. The dividends were rare but the payment of interest mounted. *C'est la vie,* as the French say.

He walked across the street to the parking lot called the *Palace.* Beth too had affairs. He was sure of it. At this point, it didn't matter. He stopped to remember on which floor he had parked. When the elevator came, he punched 5. As the door closed, his thoughts turned to Nicole. He was moments away from an evening of... The elevator arrived at his floor. He felt like a schoolboy. Excited for what was to come. He went down the aisles of cars until he came to his BMW convertible. It was a very good-looking car. Maybe he'd keep it. *Who knows?* The door opened to his touch. The car had that new leather smell. As he climbed into the driver's seat, he inhaled. *Beautiful.* He put his foot on the brake and pushed the ignition switch.

Chapter Two

Detective Jack Sheppard from Bomb and Arson was enjoying an early dinner at 5:30 p.m. He was about to bite into his corned beef and pastrami sandwich when his phone went off. He held the sandwich near his mouth, undecided whether to take a bite or answer the phone. He went for the bite.

"Aren't you going to check your phone?" Billy Dee Jackson asked.

"What's it to you?" Sheppard said, "you're retired."

"Yeah but…"

Sheppard gave him a look and then defeated, put his sandwich down. "You got to admit, Billy Dee, this is the best goddamn sandwich."

"Guaranteed heartburn." Billy Dee laughed and took a forkful of salad.

"What's with you? You leave the department and now you're on a health kick?"

"Hey," Billy Dee dropped his fork and leaned closer. "It's the wife. What can I tell you? Since the day I retired, she's been worse than the meanest SOB sergeant on the force. She watches everything and I mean e-v-e-r-y-t-h-i-n-g."

Sheppard went for the sandwich. "Sorry to hear."

"The phone, Shep."

"Damn it, Billy Dee, can't I enjoy this gastronomical delight in peace. Jesus, you've become your wife." He sighed. Then he grabbed his phone. There were three messages. He read the first one. "Shit. Bomb and Arson, a car blew up in a parking lot on La Salle. Hell."

"Guess you won't have time to finish that," Billy Dee pointed to Sheppard's plate.

"Neither do you," he said as he got up, "you're coming with."

"What?"

"Come on, Billy Dee, after your heroics with that baseball pitcher, you walk on water. It will do you good. Get you out of your wife's hair."

Billy Dee took a second or two before he answered. "Sure, okay." He then grabbed what was left of the sandwich. "Can't let something like this go to waste."

"You son of a gun."

Chapter Three

Beth was in the kitchen. It was 6:00 p.m. She wore a long button-down shirt taken from Sonny's closet and nothing else. She opened the refrigerator. "Don't you have any diet Coke?"

"Vhatever. I don't know." He shrugged.

"Jesus, Sonny, the mortgage I'm paying for this place is an arm and a leg. The least you can do…"

"Yah, yah." He strolled out of the bedroom dressed only in a pair of boxer shorts. He grabbed and kissed her. "Is not better than your diet?"

She caught her breath. "It is but I'm thirsty." She kicked the refrigerator door closed. "But maybe that can wait." She leaned into him.

He turned his head.

"What?" She asked.

"I lead." He grabbed her and kissed her hard.

"You sure do, wow." Her breath quickened. She looked down and saw he had poked through his briefs. "And you're ready to go again. Incredible." She touched him. "Hmm, more fun. Let's do it and have music." She flicked on the radio. Instead of jazz, an announcer cut in with a news bulletin of a fire in a parking garage on La Salle Street.

She froze. "Sonny, turn on the TV, hurry."

"What? I thought what we're doing—building a fire."

"Sony…please."

"Okay, I'll turn on damn set."

Even though she was tense, she couldn't take her eyes off his thirty-year-old butt.

He went to the TV. "Where is clicker? What the hell?"

"You live here. I think it's on the couch."

"Oh yeah. Got it," and pressed On. The picture showed flames licking the sides of the garage. Crews on ladders and from three trucks sprayed water on the building. The scene then switched to an interview with the fire commander.

"Oh my God." Beth sat down next to him. "What do you think happened?"

"The news say big explosion on fifth floor," he read off his phone.

"Jesus." She leaned toward the TV. Her eyeglasses were probably in the bedroom. "That's the lot where scumbag parks."

"Who?"

She felt her cheeks flush. "You know, Joe."

He looked at her puzzled, then said, "Oh…him." He moved closer and let his hand brush against her thigh.

"No… Sonny, I shouldn't. I have to listen…" She didn't move away.

He ran his fingers on the outside of her shirt and then unbuttoned the first four.

"Sonny." Her voice was thick. "I… what if…"

She felt him touch her breasts and then oh so lightly massage them.

She was on the verge of being swept away. Should she stop? Should she… oh God. She threw her head back. Her shirt spread open and Sonny's mouth replaced his hands. He was so damn good. It almost wasn't fair. "S-o-n…" she was able to get out in between his alternating kisses of her breasts and then her mouth. She turned to meet him and caught a glimpse of a person being wheeled from the building on the TV.

"Holy shit," she said.

Sonny moved down her body and accelerated the pace.

"N-o-o-o." She pulled his hair. He must not have understood. "Sonny, stop, p-l-e-a-s-e."

He was between her legs. *What the hell?* She gave up stopping the mounting surge. Whatever happened on La Salle could wait. This… She closed her eyes and allowed an *ahhh* to escape from her throat. Sonny took her away.

A little more than an hour later, Beth cabbed back to her apartment. She still throbbed from her evening's affair. In the darkened back seat of the taxi, she knew she was smiling. Glad that she had met Sonny. Glad that he stayed in her *pied-à-terre*. It was the least she could do for someone who did so, much for her. She took a breath. The cab turned onto her street.

"Mrs. Daniels," Peter, the doorman, said as she hurried past him and through the security door. "Mrs. Daniels, your…husband…"

That was all she heard as she stepped into the elevator and pressed 36. The door closed. She played the doorman's voice in her head. The last remembrance of the warmth of Sonny's touches and kisses was replaced with the coldness of the present. "Shit, what about my husband?" The floors swept by slowly for her. "Come on, come on." Finally, 36 was displayed and the elevator door opened. She hurried down the hallway to her door. She fumbled through her purse for the key. Memories of Joe scolding her as she sloshed through her things flashed through her mind. *"Prepare,"* he'd say, *"think ahead."* He'd have that frown and his bulging eyes look that she grew to hate. She found her key in her coat pocket and opened the door.

Things looked in order, as they should be. She went to the phone and saw the message light flash. *Oh God.* She steeled herself and picked up the receiver. She pressed Play.

"I'll be home late. Don't wait up."

She looked at the phone and broke into a laugh.

Chapter Four

The scene at 7:00 p.m. at the Palace garage on La Salle was chaotic. Fireman, paramedics, and detectives from Bomb and Arson swarmed around and through the building. Detective Sheppard and Billy Dee waited until the fire was under control before they went to the fifth floor. The elevators were out, so they took the stairs.

"If I'd had known I was going to climb five stories, I never would have eaten that corned beef sandwich," Sheppard said.

Billy Dee shook his head between gasps of air. "Yeah you would. You're a glutton, and why am I here? I should be home right now. What am I doing?"

Sheppard stopped a few stairs ahead. "It's in your blood, Billy Dee. You love this."

Billy Dee motioned with his hand that his partner should continue to climb. They reached the fifth floor. It was drenched in water and oil. The smell of gasoline mixed with leftover smoke pervaded the area.

"Watch your step," someone in a protective fire raincoat said. "It's slippery and the power for the lights is out."

The smoldering ruins of several cars were parked on the west side of the garage.

"That's one hell of a burnt-up car," Detective Sheppard said as he spun the toothpick in his mouth.

Billy Dee bent down to see underneath the hulk. "Yep, sure is." He stepped closer.

"What are you looking for?"

"For starters, a license plate." He moved to the front. "A VIN, something that can identify this mess." He shined his flashlight.

"Wait until the ET boys get done with it."

Billy Dee glanced up. "Yeah, you're right. Anyone hurt?"

"The beat guys said they took someone out of a BMW convertible."

"Did they talk to him?"

"Didn't say. There's the Beamer a few slots down."

They walked to what was left of the BMW convertible. The driver's door rested on the cement floor. The windows were blown out. The seats were burnt and covered in soot.

"That's one lucky dude," Billy Dee said.

"I think what saved him was the car in between, although when it burst into flames…"

"Where was he taken?"

Sheppard took out his pad and examined his notes. "Northwestern. It was the closest."

"Any other witnesses? Victims?."

"No others have been reported according to the beat cops."

Billy Dee took a breath. "Let's call the hospital and see what's what."

Sheppard nodded. "Hold on I'll take a few pictures with my phone for my file. I'm sure the Beamer guy would like to see the remains of his car."

"You're such a thoughtful man," Billy Dee said, "Hopefully there's enough left of him to pay attention."

Chapter Five

Nicole checked the wine. Joe liked red, usually a cabernet. Her taste ran more toward chardonnay, viognier, and other whites, but it kept Joe happy. She felt the bottle to make sure it was at room temperature. She opened the wine and set it on the kitchen table to breathe.

She was quick and good at her job. In the fifteen minutes since she'd gotten home, she'd showered, changed into tight jeans and a loose-fitting top, and applied the finishing touches to her eyeliner and blush. Joe expected no less. He was punctual. She sat at the table, checked the time, and eyed the wine. He'd arrive in ten minutes. She knew he was married. She found that enticing. Give men a smile and show them a little t and a, and, well… She glanced at the silver and sapphire bracelet she always wore on nights like these. She refused to think herself a gold digger, but a good life cost. She was blessed with brains and looks. She heeded the advice given at her law school commencement: "Use your potential." Success in law depended on who you knew rather than what you knew. Joe had one hell of a Rolodex.

She sighed and stretched her long legs. Her one-bedroom apartment was on the twenty-fifth floor of Delaware and State on Chicago's Gold Coast. Not bad for a girl who'd emigrated by herself from Serbia when she was sixteen. Her parents stayed in the old country. An aunt took her in. She was a quick study of American culture and the American way. Her apartment, all bought and paid for by herself.

Okay, if she was honest, she did get some help from others, but she engineered it. She had bigger wants and Joe was just the latest means of getting there.

Hmm, he was late—five minutes late. She opened her phone and re-read his e-mail. Yep, he wrote, "6:30." *Well there's always a first.* Ten more minutes went by. She got up and walked into the living room and puffed the pillows on the couch. This was strange. She was sure he hadn't lost interest. His excuses to stop by her office, or the way he'd brush against her and hoped no one saw. She had seen that look in his eyes. He had made it clear what he wanted… always wanted. She opened her phone again. There was a bulletin from CNN, CBS, and the third was WBBM: *An explosion at a LaSalle street parking lot. OMG.* That's why he's late. He was caught in traffic. She went into the kitchen and poured herself a glass. It was good, but her choice would have been better.

Chapter Six

Beth put the phone down and decided to take a hot bath. It was 8:30 p.m. She drew the water. Joe would be home soon. His image evaporated like the steam from the tub. She stepped in and the warm water crept over her body. She relaxed and closed her eyes. The evening with Sonny began to play. She was getting to the good part when the phone rang. *Good God, who would be calling at this hour?* She splashed around for the phone that hung on the wall.

"Hello?" She said.

"I'm sorry to bother you Ms. Daniels, but there are two detectives who would like to speak with you," Peter the doorman said.

"Detectives? What? Why? I'm taking a bath."

"Yes, ma'am, but they say it's important."

She clutched the phone. "Okay, okay, send them up in five minutes. I've got to get dressed."

"Thank you, Ms. Daniels, will do."

But it was barely a minute later before there was a knock on the door. She threw on a housecoat and didn't quite zip it closed.

"Hello?" She said.

"Chicago Police, please open the door."

She undid the lock and stared at a man and a woman in plain clothes.

The police officers stepped into the apartment's hallway, forcing Beth to step back.

"What's this about?" she asked.

The woman, who had blonde hair pulled back in a bun, said, "We'd like to talk to you."

Beth led them into the living room, flicked on a lamp, and slumped into a chair. "Is it Joe? Is he okay?" Her eyes blinked as if she willed her tears.

The detectives exchanged glances. "No, this is not about Joe," the male officer said.

"No?" Beth asked as her housecoat uncovered a portion of her leg. "He's alright?"

"Joe is your…?"

"He's my husband."

Both detectives wrote something down. The woman leaned forward. "Do you know an Anatoly Dmursic?"

"Who?"

The woman flipped through several pages in her notebook. "Ever see this person?" She held up a color photograph.

Beth stared at it. "That's Sonny." She bit her lip. "What happened to Sonny?" Her voice rose.

"He's dead," the woman said. "He was found in his apartment shot and with several stab wounds."

"Oh no," rose from Beth's throat and built to a scream, "*nooo*". Tears fell as she covered her face.

The detectives went toward her. "Ma'am, you'll have to come with us. You were recognized by a neighbor leaving his apartment earlier this evening." The woman put her arm around Beth and steered her toward the bedroom. "Get dressed."

Chapter Seven

Paris, May 2016

Monsieur Dumond sat in the back of the bar at the hotel Le Jeu de Paume. It was midafternoon and the place was near empty. He enjoyed the quiet. He went into his coat pocket and retrieved his pack of Gauloises. He tapped a cigarette on the table and picked up his gold lighter.

"Monsieur," the waiter rushed over. "Smoking is forbidden." The waiter's accent was not Parisian.

Dumond eyed his drink and then the cigarette in his hand. "Why? No one is here."

The waiter shrugged. "It's not me. It's the law. I would let you, but…" The shrug was pure French.

At another time, Dumond or his other aliases Jacques Benes or Andre Clique' would not have complied. But why create a scene? There was no reason. He put the cigarette back in the pack.

"Merci," the waiter said.

Dumond lifted his drink. The cognac was balanced, smooth in taste and dark in color. Appreciation of fine things was a talent he possessed. But, there was always a cost. He took another sip. He had learned that the best way to enjoy what he liked was to have others, knowingly or not, pay for them. The police used terms of forger, dealer, or smuggler to describe him. He got to know the flics well. They were good at accusing, but not in proving. *Alors,* witnesses would forget or were lost, and there were times the officer on the case couldn't find the so-called evidence. *What money can buy. C'est la vie.*

His glass was empty and he motioned the server for another. The waiter came with the drink.

"You are not busy," Dumond said.

The waiter smiled, "No, monsieur. Most of our guests are out shopping, enjoying Paris."

"It is a good thing to do." Dumond pulled out a 20-euro note and left it on the table. "Where would one find cigars… good ones."

"There is a tabac store a few blocks away."

Dumond put another 50 euros on the table. "If you can, since it isn't…"

"Oh, I don't know. I'm working."

"There is no one else here," Dumond pointed out.

The waiter looked around. "Yes, you are right."

"You won't be gone long, right? Just a few blocks."

The waiter stared at Dumond and then gazed at the money. "How many do you want?"

"Only one, a Montecristo maduro."

The waiter grabbed the bills.

"Thank you," Dumond said and watched the waiter leave. He took a cigarette from the pack of Gauloises and lit it. *What could be better than cognac and a smoke?*

Chapter Eight

"I never tire of Paris, especially in September when the air is just right. Whatever the season the city bends to it. Don't you agree?"

He was an older man, dressed in a light tweed jacket. She called him Monsieur Dumond. Wind mussed his salt and pepper hair. His eyes appeared kind, but fierceness lurked behind them.

She could have been a colleague, a family friend, or his mistress. She had flowing dark hair and an angular face. She could tell he had a certain pride walking arm in arm with her in the Jardin des Tuileries. He was gracious and old world-like in his speech. They didn't rush, but their pace was more than a stroll. He turned to her as if talking about the flowers. "*Vous irez à Chicago. Votre nom sera Susan Marks. Voici votre passeport.* (You will go to Chicago. Your name will be Susan Marks. Here is your passport.)"

"*Pourquoi?*"

He smiled as if she asked about the weather, or the wine they'd had at lunch.

"*Il est votre travail. Le mien est de planifier.* (It is your job. Mine is to plan.)"

"*Pour combien de temps vais-je être loin?* (For how long will I be away?)"

He pulled her closer as they continued their walk. "*Jusqu'à ce que je vous dis de revenir.* (Until I tell you to come home.)"

She opened the passport and stared at the picture. "*Mon*

Dieu, je suis âgé de trente-sept ans. D'où je viens? (My God, I am thirty-seven years old? Where am I from?)"

He switched to English. "Corsica, the birthplace of Napoleon."

"But I'm from Avignon."

He nodded. "Corsica's record-keeping is not like France or Germany. Papers are…" He shrugged. "They are or aren't." He patted his pocket. "*Argent.*" (Money.)

She smiled and repeated that word.

They came to a bench and sat. She dropped the passport in her purse. He leaned and whispered further instructions. She thought *un homme du monde,* a man of the world, making his lover smile. It was none of that.

Chapter Nine

Chicago, September, 2016

Susan flew to Chicago as Dumond instructed. She didn't know much about the city other than stories in *Le Monde*, and magazines like *Vogue* and *Paris Match*. The old image of Chicago of the 20s and 30s pictured with gangsters like Al Capone were vaguely remembered. It was replaced by stories of Michael Jordan and le grande basketball, and something about a goat, and the lovable Cubs, a Chicago baseball team.

She put her dark shades on and leaned back in her seat. She had two weeks to become this person…Susan. *Au revoir* to those other names she had used, but going back to Simone Dubois from the south of France was not an option. The loveliness of the countryside was the opposite of her home life. Her father drank and her mom was always afraid. Mother was from Morocco, and Father reminded her that he could send her back. Was she fifteen when she ran away? What does it matter? She found the streets of Marseilles and Paris safer than home. The school of survival was her education. She excelled at adapting. She could look like a twenty-something or a waif of fourteen. She learned languages, including English. She cleaned homes and then robbed them. She had been a mistress to many, but a lover to few. To Dumond, she was both.

The pilot interrupted her thoughts. "*Bonjour*, we will be flying at 35,000 feet. The weather in Chicago is a warm; 40 degrees…"

She stopped listening.

She met Monsieur Dumond, although at that time he went by Jacques Benes, in Geneva, Switzerland. She smiled and felt herself blush. She had been working for an elder banker, a Monsieur Goltz from Munich. She'd convinced Goltz to throw a lavish party at his estate outside of Bern, Switzerland. Goltz introduced her to all of his guests. His arm was never far from her bare back. Not only was she beautiful, but she had also persuaded Goltz to adorn her with a two-carat diamond ring and earrings, a sapphire and diamond bracelet, and a gold necklace. "*Mon cher*," she said, "don't look so anxious. I will take good care of these jewels."

He kissed her. "My darling, make sure you do not lose them. My jeweler will be very upset. They are worth a fortune even for a Swiss banker."

"Of course, and *mon cher*, you will be well rewarded."

He beamed and patted her on the ass.

"Such a lovely party," Goltz said, "they are all enjoying, even as the party nears its end."

"Heavenly," she said.

"You are the attraction of the evening."

"You are too kind." She took a step toward the glass doors that led to the outside.

"Where are you going?"

"Just for fresh air, my sweet. I want to enjoy the view and the evening. I'll be back in minutes."

"But…"

"*Mon cher*, I have not forgotten my promise of your reward."

She kissed him on the cheek and allowed him to touch her.

"Okay go, but hurry back," he said.

She walked past the other guests, to the car park and

jumped into her Puegeot. It didn't start. Benes drew along-side and told her to get in. They drove all night until they were in Germany. In the morning, they stopped at a hotel and shared a room.

"I couldn't take my eyes off of you," he said.

"Me or my jewels?"

"You."

She undid her earrings. "Why are you smiling?"

"Because, *ma petite*, you think Monsieur Goltz allowed you to wear real diamonds."

"What do you mean?"

"I mean he duped you."

"What?" She looked at the glistening earring in her hand.

Jacques reached into his pocket. "These are the real ones. They were in his safe. The lock cried out to be opened. I couldn't refuse." He took from his pocket other jewels—a gold brooch and a ruby- and diamond-filled bracelet. "Let me teach you the difference."

Chapter Ten

Chicago

"Why are you handcuffing me to the wall?" Beth asked. "I'm not a criminal. I don't understand."

The female detective took her partner aside, and then he undid the cuffs. She sat down across from Beth. Her partner took a seat near the door of the interrogation room. "Ms. Daniels."

Beth looked up.

"I'm Investigator Mary Jo Kerpnacki, and that's my partner Eddie O'Brien."

Beth looked around the room. It was stark. Not even a clock on the wall.

"Ms. Daniels, you are not under arrest. We brought you here so we can talk."

"What?" Beth's gaze snapped back to the female detective. "You forced me to get dressed and drove me here. I've never been in a police station. I don't know what to do."

"May I call you Beth?"

"Huh? Yeah."

"Good. Do you need to use the bathroom?"

Beth shook her head.

Kerpnacki opened the file that was in front of her. "When did you meet Anatoly Dmursic?"

The detective's voice was like white noise she filtered

out of her consciousness. *Anatoly Dmursic, was that his real name?* She and her husband were at a gala dinner honoring *who the fuck remembers.* Joe demanded her attendance. She hated to be paraded and represent the *good wife.* One after another, the speakers lavished praise on *her dumb-fuck husband.* Before it was Joe's turn to speak, she made an excuse about the lady's room and instead went to the bar.

"Beth, I'm talking to you. Dmursic?"

"Yeah, what about him?" Her voice sounded like it was coming from someone else.

"Look, if you cooperate with us, you'll probably be walking out of here soon," Kerpnacki said.

"What? You can keep me here? For how long? Why?"

O'Brien interrupted his partner, "We've got a dead body and a witness who saw you leave the apartment. We want to know what you were doing there and why you left."

Beth looked from O'Brien to Kerpnacki, "I…I… Dmursic? He told me his name was Sonny. I don't know that other name." Her eyes welled-up. Her shoulders shook. "What… is … happening…? I'm… a…..good… per…son. I…" She buried her head in her arms. "We…uhm…had…an…"

"You had a what?" Kerpnacki asked.

"Why…would…I kill…him?" She looked at each detective through teary eyes.

O'Brien got up and moved toward Beth. He put both hands on the table and leaned inches from Beth's face. "Dmursic was a bad guy. He was into guns and drugs but we believe that was a cover. So, straighten yourself out and tell us what you know."

"Can I have a tissue?" Beth rubbed the tears from her face and wiped her nose with her hand.

The detectives glanced at each other. "Sure," O'Brien said. "Maybe milk and cookies too?"

Chapter Eleven

Nicole drank half the bottle. Joe was now an hour late. *Men. They get dazzled by a new toy and then lose interest when they see something newer.* Joe was never tardy and traffic was no longer an excuse. *Shit.* She eyed her cell. *Should she call? What if he's with another woman or hell, his wife? Damn that's the awkwardness of affairs. Easy to get in…* She smiled. *So easy.* She had learned that Joe Daniels was smart and rich. His clients were criminals, usually the white-collar types as well as individuals that made Chicago hum along with a slathering of corporations. Zoning issues, problems with the City or the State, vanished with a few phone calls.

She picked up her phone and punched in his number. Her finger hovered over Send. She didn't want to come across as the *bitchy woman*, too much like a wife. On the other hand, she did play the part of the concerned girlfriend, and co-worker. She put the phone down and brushed a strand of hair from her face. She had planned and calculated her entrée into his firm. She built her own dossier on him, and then attended the same social gatherings. The poor dear, as smart as he was, never knew he was being played.

She poured more wine but swallowed the cabernet too quickly and went into a coughing fit. A drink of water ended the spasm. Her kitchen suddenly felt cold. The tips of her fingers and toes tingled as she caught her breath. *What if he knew? What if it was she who was being played? Oh my God.* She drummed her fingers on the table. *How did I fuck up? Anatoly Dmursic? Did that son-of-a-bitch tip off his dumb-ass wife? I warned him to be careful.* She shouldn't jump to conclusions. She got this far because she was good at what she did.

She went to her bedroom and opened a deep desk drawer. She dug through a pile of papers until she found the phone. She convinced herself this was an emergency and made the call.

"Allo, Anatoly," she said in fluent Serbian.

"Chello, why you calling me?" He answered in the same language.

"Joe hasn't shown up," she said. "Is everything all right with the wife?"

"Joe?" he laughed, "He was in parking lot that blew up. He at Northwestern. And yes, evening went well with wife… very well."

"Good, keep it that way," Nicole said.

"Don't vorry, I vill. I've got to go, someone at door."

"Don't be stupid, Anatoly."

"Yah, you tell me that. So far so good. Bye."

She put the phone back and returned to the kitchen. At least no one had screwed up…yet. *Might as well finish the glass.* The taste of the wine had improved. She could get to like reds.

Chapter Twelve

Joe was strapped to a gurney and rolled into the back of the ambulance.

"You're going to be okay," he heard someone say.

That's movie talk. The last scene of *Butch Cassidy and the Sundance Kid,* flashed by. Shit, he's going to die. He groaned. *What the hell happened?* He got into his car…

"Can you tell me your name? What's your name?" The voice was female.

What a nice voice. I know my name. Can a dead person talk? "My name is J-o-e, … D-a-n…" *Hell I'm not dead.*

"You're doing good…"

He mouthed the last part of his name.

"That's okay."

He was not a religious man. He hadn't used the Deity's name other than to curse since he was a teen. God let me score. God let me win. But today, at this moment, he moved his lips and implored God to save him. He wasn't ready to be in the past tense.

"We want to make your breathing easier," the woman said.

He felt cold air on his face. It took seconds? minutes? for him to realize a mask covered his mouth. He tried to move his head. *Where were his hands, his feet?* He couldn't feel them.

***

"Blood pressure is dropping," Lucy, the female paramedic said to her partner, James. She touched Joe's skin.

James reached for the intravenous equipment.

"His skin is clammy. Jesus he's breathing like he's running a marathon," she said.

"Let's hook him up," James said. "He needs fluids. He's going into shock.

What's the time?"

"Damn, about 6:15 p.m."

***

Something pricked his arm, but Joe didn't know what it was nor cared. There was a crowd around a car, wait… his car. "Yeah that's mine," he yelled. At first, he couldn't see who these people were. "Get away from there." They didn't move.

"Joe, do you hear me?"

He had heard that voice before. Where?

"Come on back, Joe."

He must have opened his eyes.

"I thought we lost you," the woman who'd asked his name said.

He shut his eyes. The crowd was still there. A person came from somewhere, he couldn't tell where. She spoke.

"I know you," he said.

She laughed. "You should you bastard."

"What's his heart rate?" James asked.

"Dropping to 95," Lucy said.

"Shit."

"Beth? What are you doing here? Where are you going? Jesus, what's happening?"

Beth morphed into a man. He had blond hair and was husky.

"Who the fuck are you?" Joe asked.

He opened his mouth and had rows of shining teeth.

***

"What's it now? James asked.

"93," answered Lucy.

"How much farther to the hospital?"

"It's still rush hour. No one cares about the fuck'n siren."

James reached into his medical bag. "If the number doesn't go up in a minute or two, I'll give him a shot of epinephrine"

***

Joe heard water. *Where could that be coming from. He was in a garage.* "Nicole, baby I'll take you for a ride. You'll love this car." She was in a bikini. "Come on, let's go." She stepped aside and a wave came crashing over him. He shivered from the wetness and cold. "Where did you go? Nicole?"

"Here, take this." A man and a woman held out a box.

"I don't understand?" Joe said.

"It's for you," she said.

"But I don't even know you."

"But we know you." She put the box in his hand.

He pried open the top with his fingers.

The couple stepped back.

"Hey, what is this?" he shouted. He looked into the container and saw something metal.

"One, two, three, boom," she said.

***

"Hey his BP is over 100 and stabilizing," Lucy reported. "Good job."

Chapter Thirteen

Billy Dee sat in the passenger seat as Sheppard drove to Northwestern Hospital the day after the explosion. "You know, this is a beautiful city if you don't go west of Lake Shore Drive."

"I don't know about that, Billy Dee, a lot of the city has gotten better."

"Well, much of it has gotten worse. There are neighborhoods…forget it. It is what it is."

The traffic crawled going north.

"While we're breathing fumes, let me run a check on our victim. Give me your notebook."

Sheppard flipped the book out of his jacket pocket. "Have fun. Hope you can read my handwriting."

"Why, are you a doctor or something?" Billy Dee flipped opened the pages. He moved it back and forth.

"Having problems?"

Billy Dee put on his glasses. "Much better." He brought the page closer to his face. "Is that a 'J' or a…"

"Let me see that." Sheppard took the book out of Billy Dee's hand.

"You're driving."

"No, I'm stalled in traffic. The victim's name is Joe Daniels."

Billy Dee flicked on the police computer attached to the dash. He typed in the name and the date of birth Sheppard read off.

"Well?" Sheppard asked.

"So far he's clean. No record, not even a traffic ticket. He does live in expensive digs, not far from the hospital."

"So why do you think he got blown up?" Sheppard asked.

"Wrong place at the wrong time."

"Nah, that's real bad luck."

"Hmm, a business transaction gone bad," Billy Dee said while looking at the scenery.

"I don't get that vibe, but…"

"How about the old stand-by… I heard the French have a say'n, 'cherchez la femme.' Look for the woman."

"French? When did you get so urbane, Billy Dee?"

"I'm a very cultured man." He gave Sheppard a fuck-you smile.

For no apparent reason, traffic opened, and ten minutes later they arrived at the hospital.

"Did I tell you I hate hospitals? Billy Dee said.

"Really. I keep learning things about you I never knew."

"Just wanted to make a point. I'm doing you a big favor by going in here."

"I'll note it in the report."

They parked and went into the hospital. They went up to the bomb victim's room.

"Mr. Daniels, I'm Detective Sheppard and this is Investigator Billy Dee Jackson."

The man in the bed was swathed in bandages and connected to intravenous tubes. There were machines attached to him that were beeping and had numbers flashing.

"Mr. Daniels, do you hear me? Nod if you do."

The patient didn't move.

Billy Dee moved around the bed.

"What the hell are you doing?" Sheppard asked.

Billy Dee held up his finger in a gesture to wait. He grabbed the medical chart that was in a sleeve attached to the bed. He looked at the first page. "This isn't Mr. Daniels."

"Huh? Let me see."

Sheppard looked over Billy Dee's shoulder. The name typed on the first line of the chart was Angelo DeRose, a burn victim.

"So where the hell is Daniels?" Sheppard asked. "Intake said they brought him to 2033 yesterday. This is 2033, isn't it?"

Billy Dee nodded. "Yep, I checked it and I'll do it again." He stepped into the hall. "That's what's on the door."

"Crap." Sheppard looked around the room.

"There's no one else here," Billy Dee said.

"I can see that. It's reflex. Sometimes there's a bed 'A' and a bed 'B'."

"Uh huh, well, here there's only a bed."

"Got it." Sheppard moved toward the doorway. "Sorry to have bothered you, Mr. DeRose." The man in the bed didn't respond.

Sheppard met Billy Dee who was already down the hall. "Damn, let's go to Admitting."

Chapter Fourteen

Beth stared at her interrogators. "Look, I don't know anything more about Anatoly Dmursic. You've kept me here long enough. It feels like days."

"Okay, if that's the way you're playing it," O'Brien said. He turned to his partner, Kerpnacki, "We'll keep her locked in the cell."

"Huh?" Beth said.

Kerpnacki stood behind Beth. "Get up and put your hands behind your back."

"You can't be serious. You're putting me back… in jail?"

"That's right, honey. Right now, you're our prime suspect."

"I have a right to a call," Beth said, as Kerpnacki grabbed her arm. "I have a constitutional…"

"Yeah, we heard you. You'll be given the chance."

"But…I want my lawyer, my husband, Joseph Daniels."

Kerpnacki had one arm cuffed. "Who?"

Beth twisted her body toward Kerpnacki. "Joe Daniels. I've told you that."

Kerpnacki undid the cuff.

"Sit down, Beth," O'Brien said, "let's start from the beginning." He looked at his partner. "Maybe Beth would like something to drink?"

"Coffee? Water? A can of cola?" Kerpnacki asked,

"A shower but if I can't have that, a cola." Beth said.

The detective left. O'Brien took a seat across from the prisoner.

"We got off on the wrong foot," O'Brien said.

"You think?"

"Your husband is Joe Daniels… the lawyer?"

"One and the same. Can I go now?"

"Well," he drew a deep breath, "doesn't make a difference. The witness saw Dmursic lying in a pool of blood right after you left the apartment. Do you own a gun?"

"Huh?"

"What part of the question don't you understand?"

"No." She folded her hands into the other.

"No, what?"

"I don't own a gun."

"You have a firearms identification card."

"Is that supposed to be a question?"

"Yes."

"Obviously, you know I do, but I don't own a gun."

"What about your husband?"

"Joe?" A brief smile crossed her face. "He may, I really don't know."

The detective's expression was of disbelief.

"Look, Detective," Beth leaned closer to O'Brien, "our marriage isn't the greatest. Most of the time, I don't know what Joe is doing or where. So, it's possible he has a gun."

Kerpnacki returned to the room. "Diet Pepsi is all the machine had."

Beth peeled the top and took a drink. She made a face. "Ugh, diet is for shit." She gazed at the two detectives. "Excuse my language," she paused, "I don't have more to tell you, and that's the God's truth."

"Good to know," O'Brien said, "but you still haven't told us what you were doing with Dmursic. Or why you have an FOID card?"

"Jesus, alright, Dmursic was an acquaintance."

"A what?" O'Brien asked.

"An acquaint…"

O'Brien stared at her.

"Okay, I'm allowed to have a friend. My husband is gone all day and most of the night… I…eh… he's just a pal, Sonny."

"So how long you've been knowing Sonny, your buddy."

Beth took another swig and burped. "Sorry, diet does that to me."

"No problem. You were saying…"

"I was saying…? I wasn't saying." Beth looked from one detective to the other.

Kerpnacki took out an official-looking document from a folder. "You know what this is?" She put the document in front of Beth.

Beth looked down and let out a small gasp. She covered her mouth. "Where did you get this?"

"That's your name on the deed."

Beth picked up the paper with the official stamp from the Recorder of Deeds and looked at it closely. Then dropped it on the table. She stared at Kerpnacki and then O'Brien. "I have money and I invest in real estate."

"Come on, Beth, we're all grown-ups here. Stop bullshit-ting," O'Brien said.

Beth wiped her face with her hands and said in a defeated voice, "Okay, I had an affair. Joe didn't know about the apartment or him."

"Did he pay rent?" O'Brien asked.

"He…eh…what difference does that make."

"Well, did he?"

"No." Beth took a breath. "I told him he could use the place for as long as he wanted."

"Did you catch him cheating?" O'Brien asked.

"Joe?"

"No, your Sonny."

"Was he?"

"That's what I'm asking."

"Not that I knew. Really, it was just an affair, and it was going well."

O'Brien put on a glove and reached into a large opaque envelope. "This was recovered down the hall from where Dmursic or Sonny was shot." He held a blue steel Beretta Px4 compact. "Ever see this before?" He brought it closer to Beth.

"That…this? No… I don't own a gun. I don't like them. Please, I'm afraid of them."

"So, you've never seen this weapon before?"

"On my life…never."

"What would you call this gun?"

She looked up. "What do you mean? It's a semi-aut…"

"Automatic. You're right. It's a semi-automatic pistol and guess who it's registered to."

Chapter Fifteen

Billy Dee and Detective Sheppard stood before the woman in charge of hospital admittance.

"We can't disclose patient information. Read the HIPAA rules." She wiped her eye glasses with a tissue.

The two men didn't move.

She dropped her specs on the desk.

"HIPAA?" Sheppard asked more to Billy Dee than to the woman.

She tucked at the sleeve of her suit coat, pulling it over the cuff of her blouse.

"I've heard of it, but…" Billy Dee looked around, "I don't see…"

"Are you kidding me?" the woman asked. "It's against the privacy rules of patients."

"Oh, got it," Billy Dee said. "You know, ma'am, Mr. Daniels was brought here by ambulance… a Chicago Fire Department ambulance, property of the City of Chicago. Yesterday, your personnel told us that Mr. Daniels was taken to room 2033. The doctor told us we couldn't see him last night. We came today. He's not there."

The woman placed both her palms on the desk and looked directly at both officers. "Gentlemen, I can't do anything for you. Unless you have a subpoena or you are family, I can't…"

"Yeah, yeah, you've said that," Sheppard said stroking a non-existent beard. "What does that sound like to you, Billy Dee?"

"Well, we're investigating a bombing. The victim is missing from the hospital, and this lady who has the information seems to be, what's the word?"

"Obstructing," Sheppard said.

"That's it, you could say she's interfering with a police investigation."

"I'm what?" she asked

"Isn't that a felony, Shep?"

The woman reached for the phone.

Billy Dee put his hand on top of hers. "All you have to do is tell us where he is."

The woman took her hand away. Her face was flushed. "This is outrageous. I have never…" She put her glasses on. "You're threatening me with arrest?"

Billy Dee smiled, "No, lady, you're talking yourself into it. Just give us the information."

She turned to her computer and typed in a code. The patient's name appeared. She read out loud, "Daniels was brought in yesterday and discharged an hour ago."

"He was?" Billy Dee said. "Who picked him up? Who was he discharged to?"

The woman stood. "I gave you what you wanted. Get the hell out of here."

Billy Dee looked at Sheppard. "Let's go with the obvious and find the wife."

Back in their car, Billy Dee asked, "I thought he was in bad shape?"

"That's what the paramedics told me."

"Huh. Maybe the wife didn't like the hospital. Or his personal physician didn't have privileges at Northwestern."

Sheppard gave him a look. "Come on, Billy Dee you haven't been away from this crap that long. Something stinks."

"See, that's why you need me."

"Yeah?"

"I bring a more positive outlook. I have faith."

"Oh, man, a reformed cop. God help me."

"Hold on, I'm just say'n there could be other possibilities."

"We'll soon find out. His address is on the printout."

They drove down a few streets until they came to Chestnut.

"That's the apartment building," Sheppard said. It was a high-rise steps from the lake.

"Fancy digs," Billy Dee said.

They double-parked in front and strode through the building's revolving door. The security attendant, a small man wearing a blue sport coat with the name of the building sewed on it, was seated at the desk.

"Can I help you?" the attendant asked. His nametag of Peter was clipped to his upper pocket.

Sheppard flashed his badge. "We'd like to talk to Mrs. Daniels.

Peter lurched backward as if he was struck. "Mrs. Daniels?"

"Yes, Mrs. Beth Daniels."

"I don't understand."

"You don't understand? Now we don't get it. We're police officers and want to talk to one of your tenants. Simple. Is she at home?"

"Detectives, I… uh… she was picked up by two other officers last night."

"She was? Are you sure?"

"I'm been at this job a long time. I'm telling you she's already with the police."

Chapter Sixteen

Nicole went to work at Joe's law firm the next day. The office gossip was all about Joe. He was in the hospital. *Should I visit? What about his wife?* Joe's personal secretary seemed to think his injuries weren't life-threatening. *Maybe he will call or ...*jeez. Nicole left the office early and went home. She slipped into something loose and attacked the leftover wine from last night.

She got up from the table and stepped to the floor-to-ceiling windows in the living room. She had a sweeping north view of the city. The lights of the tall buildings glowed. It was a view made of money, beckoning anyone with enough smarts and balls. She stepped back and flicked on a lamp. The silver sapphire bracelet on her arm caught the light.

She was nearing thirty. Life had not been boring, but adventure had its own issues. Living on the edge came with a growing awareness. She looked at the city laid out before her. What sparkles can also dim or be taken away.

She usually worked these schemes alone. It was safer, cleaner, and in most cases more profitable. Her scam was simple but effective—blackmail. A little affair, push for marriage, and when the mark said he couldn't, or wouldn't, "Well, honey, nothing is free in this world."

Her plan was working. She got Joe to hire her and then fall for her. But no design can prepare for every event, especially unforeseen. She hadn't figured Joe would be at the Palace Garage at the wrong time.

Anatoly.

The crazy son-of-a-bitch changed everything. He'd come into her life months before, at a dinner honoring Joe. She had stepped into the bar and saw this man, who she later found out to be Anatoly, do more than talk to Joe's wife. His hands were all over her, fellow drinkers be damned.

From her experience in affairs, Joe's wife was either starting or wanting one. She played with the idea of a double blackmail. Of course, it could all backfire, but the rewards could be better than just working alone. The price of disentangling these "matters of the heart" could be quite a gain.

She glanced out the window of her apartment and admired the twinkling lights of the city. Her glass was empty.

She thought back to that dinner and how, with a little charm and bluff, she obtained the guest list. She asked questions of the dinner chairman and in less than a week obtained Anatoly's phone number. She called and asked if he would be interested in meeting.

He agreed.

"How many conspiracies have been launched at Starbucks?" she asked him while waiting for their order.

He grinned. He took his coffee black. They sat and talked about Chicago. How long each had lived there. She watched in wonderment as he gulped his drink while steam rose from the cup.

Then she asked him about Joe's wife, Beth.

He smiled. "She is like dog in heat. She look for good time."

"Really? How do you know?"

He gave her a long look. "Men know just like you know vit him. I saw where this Joe was looking."

She must have blushed. Her face felt warm. "Why, thank you," she said in a southern drawl that was lost on him.

For a minute or two, neither said a word. "You know," Nicole began…

"Yah, I know, it could vork for both of us."

That was the start of their plan. A week or two later, Anatoly called and asked to meet at another Starbucks.

"I have propozition," he said. His eyes twinkled as they found a table in the back.

"What kind of proposition?"

"Dis lawyer, Joe Daniels…"

"Not so loud."

"Yah, Joe, he a big shot, yes?"

She nodded.

"He knows many people?"

"Yeah, he's a powerful man and rich."

His dark eyes widened.

"You know he…" Anatoly turned in his seat and then back to Nicole. "Dis guy is not just lawyer."

"What do you mean?"

He motioned Nicole to come closer. "He has other businesses."

"Huh?"

"I have friend. His name is Hugo. If interested, he better to explain. If you don't want, fine, but this deal will bring more money than our little game."

She caught her breath. "I'm listening."

"This is what my friend Hugo say," Anatoly said, "he helps out, how do I say, eh, less fortunate people."

"What are you talking about?" Nicole asked. "What poor people? You saying that Joe Daniels works in soup kitchens?"

Anatoly laughed. "No, not at all." He motioned to go outside.

They left the coffee shop and started down the street.

"Hugo is Serbian like me. He been here for many years, but in Serbia, he fought in war in the 90s."

"Good for him."

Anatoly stopped. "If not interested, fine by me. I fuck Daniels' wife and play same game as you."

"No, no go ahead, sorry. Okay, Hugo is a freedom fighter, so?"

Anatoly bit his lip. "You are difficult woman. He fought for his country, so yes, Hugo is freedom fighter."

"*Dobro sto je sredeno.* Good, that's settled," she said in perfect Serbian.

"Holy fuck, how you know to say that," he said.

She smiled, "I got out at the start of the war. I was lucky."

They passed a few stores before Anatoly spoke again. "You meet with Hugo. I set it up. Better from his mouth. If you want, we'll be partners, if not, okay. I'll screw wife and you'll take care of husband, and we'll both come out."

Chapter Seventeen

Hugo never left the war between the Serbs and Croats behind, even though years, decades had past. His family had lived with other Serbs in territory controlled by the Croatians. They'd left their village and everything else behind as destruction and death tore through their hamlet. He lost his parents and sister, but he made it to Serbian territory. He was too wounded to fight. Frustrated, he turned to drink and, in one of his drunken stupors, stumbled into a ramshackle building. There were three men bent over a table. They all turned and pointed their guns. One of the men must have recognized him, another refugee from his town. They began to talk and shortly after, Hugo entered the world of weapons smuggling. He was a quick study and soon had contacts world-wide. By the mid-1990s, he emigrated to Chicago and went into the fruit and vegetable business off Lake Street in the west Loop. The warehouse didn't look like much, but it did well in hiding his real business.

***

It had turned chilly in late October. Hugo sat behind an old wooden desk in the back of his warehouse wearing a moth- eaten wool sweater. The front of the building was dark. The only light came from a hanging bulb over his desk. He checked his watch. It was almost nine p.m. This was the second time in a row that he had stayed this late. Business was picking up. His appointment now was with a woman. From the moment she came in she made it difficult for him to concentrate on the business at hand. She dressed in a skimpy t-shirt and a pair of tight-fitting jeans. She spoke with a slight French accent. There were few pleasantries besides, "Allo" and the password. She stood over the desk. "I have a client who is looking for guns that are not traceable. My source informed me you are the person who can do this."

He gazed up at her. "Before I answer, I must know who that is. So far you are two for two."

She gave him a quizzical look.

"You knew my name and the password. Now I have to know who sent you."

"Of course." She took a piece of paper from his desk and wrote down a name.

"I know this man. We had some dealings in Europe, but that was years ago. What's your relationship to him?"

She smiled. "I cannot tell you but here's what I can do. This is my number. Use the name Susan. When you're satisfied, we can do business."

She left and he had only enough time to use the bathroom before meeting Anatoly and his friend.

There was a knock. He could see from the monitor in front of him who it was. He opened the door.

"Anatoly," he said. "Welcome. It has been too long." They hugged and patted each other on the back. "And who is this?"

"This is Nicole, the voman I tell you about," Anatoly said.

Hugo switched to Serbian remarking on the attractiveness of his friend.

"She understands perfectly what you say," Anatoly said, "her Serbian is as good as mine."

Hugo looked at her and saw her face was flushed.

"Thank you for the compliment," she said, "and yes, I do have long legs."

Everyone laughed.

"Let me get some chairs. We'll share a taste. Yes?" Hugo said.

He brought out two folding chairs and then opened a desk drawer. "Vodka?" He poured three glasses. They clinked and chugged the drink. "More?" Hugo asked Nicole.

"Yes, this is a good start, but before we have another, I want to hear your proposition."

"She is direct," Hugo said, "no bullshitting. Okay. In the front of this warehouse there are crates and boxes of vegetables. It's a living, but I also have another business. Through the street I hear a name, Joe Daniels. I learn he's a big shot lawyer…. nice clothes, nice office, nice everything, but…" Hugo held up his forefinger and pointed at Nicole, "he also does deals, how do I say, off the books."

"Drugs?" Nicole asked.

"That I don't know," Hugo shrugged and leaned closer. He kept his gaze on Nicole. He stuck out his forefinger and made a motion with his thumb. "Bang bang. Your friend sells weapons. He gives the cops business by arming the gangs."

"What? Can't be. Joe? You're full of shit," Nicole said.

"Believe me or not," he shrugged. "The street talks and my information is good. I want part of that business."

"Holy crap. I had no idea." Nicole looked at Anatoly, then back to Hugo. "This is so far out of my league. I don't know."

"Anatoly told me your little game. Very nice. You make a few thousand. I'm talking hundreds of thousands."

"Hundreds of thousands?"

"Guns are big business, Nicole, and buyers pay for good, dependable weapons. They pay very well. I need to be introduced to your Joe."

"Jesus, this is illegal."

"And what you two plan isn't?"

Nicole brushed a strand of hair away from her mouth. "Immoral, maybe, but not against the law."

"I'm not lawyer," Hugo said, "legal, not legal, morality, I'm talking money…real money. We get this deal, and our futures are all good."

"That could be a frightening thought. I'm thinking about the Feds," Nicole said.

Hugo sat back and eyed the bottle of vodka. "Let's drink. Another?"

Nicole took a breath. "Why not."

"Good. Let's drink to bright futures."

"*Ziveli'* cheers." Anatoly joined Nicole and Hugo in the toast.

Hugo slammed his glass down, then got up from the chair. "Think about it. In or out, it's okay, but everything we talk stays here. This I promise, if you agree and Joe and I do business, we will be partners and share in the profits." He put his finger to his lips. "Not a word about this to anybody. Yes?"

Nicole and Anatoly nodded.

"Give me a few days," Nicole said, "I will let you know."

Chapter Eighteen

Paris

Monsieur Dumond sat on a bench in the Jardin des Tuileries. Even in late October certain flowers still bloomed. He was alone. He put his newspaper down and checked his watch: 3:00 p.m. His phone rang.

"*Oui,*" he said.

The voice on the other end was guttural and Eastern European. "We have the money. When do we get the package?"

"Monsieur, it is a lovely day. You must see what Paris is like in this season."

Static exploded on the line. Dumond pulled the phone away from his ear for a few seconds. "Allo," he said. The line cleared.

"Tuesday," the voice on the other end said.

"A week from today is good. I'll be at the Hotel Duquesne Eiffel. Say…" he glanced at his watch, "1 p.m. for lunch."

"We'll see, Frenchman. Do not disappoint us. For the money you will be getting we expect prompt delivery and excellent product."

"I satisfy my customers. You must already know this, otherwise we wouldn't be having this conversation. But I am not Amazon."

"Huh?" There was a pause. "Amazon, oh, that is a good one. Someday maybe it will replace you."

"Well, until then, Tuesday." Dumond ended the call. He gazed at the gardens. It was beautiful no matter what season of the year. He took a breath and thought to himself. *Amazon could never replace me. Matter of fact, I would have to be reinvented. This particular business requires no paper, no receipts, only cash. Credit cards are traceable. It is the last bastion of a handshake deal.* He had to laugh. Murderers, fanatics, revolutionaries, whatever they want to be called, all worked on a system of faith, fear, and death, if betrayed. It was as honest a system as any except there was no appeal or second chance to get it right.

In Chicago, it would be morning, around 8 a.m. Susan would be… He closed his eyes and pictured her getting out of bed. That face, her hair, the way she carried herself…he was violating his own rules. Jesus, it was difficult to admit, but he was fond of her. He knew it was not good business to allow emotions to creep in. It could endanger both of them. But he thought back to that night he helped her escape from the Swiss banker's home. She was so young—not naïve in the way of life, but professionally. He had taught her more than the ability to distinguish real from fake diamonds, including the know-how needed to stay alive. She was an adept student. She had it all: beautiful, sexual, and instinctual. A lethal combination.

He stared at his phone, then typed a message. "Meeting for next Tuesday, make sure the candy is available, D."

Chapter Nineteen

Chicago

"Don't that beat all," Billy Dee said, as he and Sheppard walked back to their car from Beth Daniels' apartment building. "One hand don't know from the other. See, Shep, nothing changed since I retired from the department."

"Stop your squawking. There's a bigger issue."

"Yeah I know. It ain't the wife."

Shep unlocked the undercover police vehicle and they got in. Billy Dee felt his front pocket.

"What are you looking for?"

"Huh? Since we're going to be sitting here for a few, thought I'd light my cigar. Helps me think."

"No, you're not. I don't want that stinking up the car."

"Since when you—"

Sheppard reached for his Benson & Hedges on the dash. He lit a cigarette and blew the smoke in Billy Dee's direction.

"One of those are okay, but stogies upset your delicate sense of smell? You got to be kidding." Billy Dee waved the smoke from him with one hand and continued his search with the other. He felt his shirt pocket. "Look at this beauty. All tobacco, unlike the crap you're smoking."

"I'm not in the mood for your lecture on cigars versus cigarettes. I don't like your shit, never have, never will. As far as sensitivity," he had a sheepish grin, "that"— he pointed to Billy Dee's cigar—"got me sicker than I've ever been."

"Jesus, you're worse than the wife." He put the cigar in his mouth. "I won't light the damn thing. Okay?"

A détente settled as Sheppard continued his smoke and Billy Dee chewed his unlit cigar. "Hey, this is Area North's territory," Billy Dee said, breaking the silence.

"Yeah, so?"

"You're only involved in whether there was arson at the Palace garage. Violent crimes may be investigating who put it there."

"Billy Dee, that's part of my, I mean, our job."

Billy Dee shrugged. "My bet is Violent Crimes picked the wife up. Who knows why?"

"So Violent Crimes picked her up last night? Jesus. That means those dicks are working nights." Sheppard glanced at the time – 8:30 p.m. He threw his cigarette out the window. "We should find out what the other hand is doing."

***

It took twenty minutes to get from the lakefront to Belmont and Western. The police station that housed the detective unit for Area North was located on a corner that used to house an amusement park.

"You go ahead in, Shep, I want to take my time. It's been a while since I saw this place."

"Don't get sentimental on me, Billy Dee. I know you worked here for years."

"Yeah, sure did. Hasn't changed. It's the same tired pot-holed parking lot."

Sheppard nudged him. "And it's the same tired brown brick on the inside. Come on, you didn't lose anything out here."

They entered the two-story police station but instead of stopping at the front counter at the entrance, they turned to go up the stairs to the detective units.

"Hey, where do you think you're going?" a woman shouted. She moved from behind the counter to the landing by the stairs.

"Up there," Sheppard pointed and flashed his badge, identifying him as a detective.

"Get down here. You know you can't just go where you like. Who's the other fellow with you?"

Billy Dee turned. "Sgt. McNamara, nice to see you."

Surprise registered on her face. "Billy Dee Jackson. How the hell are you? Didn't you retire a few months ago?"

"Sure did."

"And you're back already? Does your wife know?"

"Janine? Come on, Sarge… I'm just help'n my friend Detective Sheppard."

"Doing what?"

"Oh, this and that. Going to crime scenes, keeping Shep, here, on the straight and narrow," he laughed.

"Really. Remember, Billy Dee you aren't on the force anymore."

"Got you."

McNamara shifted her attention. "Who do you want to see, Detective?"

"Not sure. I'm working on that explosion in the La Salle Street parking lot, and I'm trying to find the wife of the victim." He took out his notebook. "Beth Daniels."

"Give me a minute, and I'll check," the sergeant said.

They all went back to the front counter. McNamara went behind the barrier and picked up the phone. After a short conversation, she returned.

"Homicide is talking to her. Detectives O'Brien and Kerpnacki are the ones assigned. One of them will come down."

Billy Dee shot Sheppard a look. "Joe Daniels died? Maybe that explains his leaving the hospital."

Sheppard shook his head. "That ain't it."

"Boys, you'll just need to wait. Have a seat," McNamara said.

Chapter Twenty

The iPhone by the bed chimed, and then went silent. Susan stirred. When the phone went off again, she lifted her head from the pillow. She glanced at the table clock and grabbed her cell. "*Mon Dieu.*" It was past 8:00 a.m. She'd overslept. She glanced at the message but didn't focus. Other thoughts crowded in. She drew the covers from her and looked. She had nothing on. She shut her eyes for a second. *Was she alone? Was there a man…a woman…* She peeked over her shoulder. *Merde,* there was a man lying near the other edge of the bed. She was now very awake. This wasn't her bedroom. She stayed to her side and searched the floor for her clothes. *What the hell happened last night?* Fragments of memory flashed through her head. *I have to get out.*

Her clothes weren't there. *They must be on his side or… God.* She slipped out of bed. She didn't feel awkward being naked in someone's bedroom. Being *au natural* was part of being French. She tiptoed around the bed. The man stirred. The door was across the room. She edged her way to it.

"Hey where… are you… going?" His voice was full of sleep.

She didn't stop. "Bathroom."

"Peeing … important. Hurry back. That French ass of yours is…" his voice drifted off, "art."

Her clothes were strewn down the hallway. She stooped to grab them. She snatched her bikini panties and bra, squished them in her hand, then slipped on her jeans and buttoned her shirt. She picked her jacket from the floor and stuffed the underwear in her pocket. She had her hand on the front doorknob, silently congratulating herself on her escape, only to realize she'd left her phone in the bedroom. *Sacre Bleu, how stupid of me. What now?* She bit her lip. She heard the floor creak and turned from the door. Her bedmate came toward her. He had a towel around his waist.

"You forgot this," he said holding her phone.

He was a good-looking man. He had age on him but he was tall, developed, but not overly. His light brown hair stuck out in all direction. He wasn't smiling, but he didn't appear angry.

"Thanks," she said, "I am late. I should be at work."

He tossed her cell on a chair and stepped closer.

"My boss will be upset."

He pulled her toward him and kissed her. Her body tingled, but she forced herself to break away. "Really, I..."

She didn't refuse his second kiss. He touched her nape and she felt his hands go slowly down her back. *Mon Dieu, it is like drifting down a path full of pleasures knowing the delights will only intensify. No, I have to leave.* His hand was at her waist. She could hear herself breathe, or was that him? *It wouldn't take much more to find myself back in bed.* She felt him cup her ass. *Non, I cannot.*

"What's a few more minutes?" He began to unbutton her shirt.

"Please...I cannot...I..."

Her resistance was smothered by another embrace. They started to move toward the bedroom as he reached the last of her buttons.

"Wait," she said. "I hear something."

"What? Where?"

"My phone. It's playing the *Marseillaise*. Someone's calling."

"What the hell? Who cares?" He cupped her breast.

"Non, wait." She slapped his hand away and went to the phone.

"Allo? Allo." She looked at the screen that said 'missed call'. She was about to check her voicemail when she felt his breath on her neck.

"Please, I must go. There will be another time." She took a small step away and began to re-button her shirt.

He grabbed her shoulder and spun her around.

Her training took over. Her kick to his groin sank him to the floor. He writhed in pain and brought his knees to his stomach.

She stood over him and then kneeled. "Hugo, this was a mistake. The bedroom shouldn't be mixed with our business. It makes everything messy. Business is business."

Hugo stayed in the fetal position.

"I only met you last week. We had fun, especially last night. Too much booze, and we both shouldn't have let it happen. It did, and it was a mistake. Errors are costly."

She walked over to the chair and picked up her cell. She read the message and listened to the voice mail from Dumond. *Thank God Hugo brought the goods last night.* She'd been at his warehouse off Lake Street when he showed her the guns secreted in his van. After she inspected the weapons, they argued over the terms, and finally settled. It led to the celebration.

She put the phone in her pocket and caught Hugo sliding toward the hallway to the bedroom.

She took a few steps toward him. "You know, maybe I was too hasty. Everything is good. Come, give me your hand." She pulled him up and helped him to his bed. "Do you think you can?"

He looked at her, confused. "I… I don't know. That was some kick." The towel had fallen off and he touched himself.

She smiled and slipped out of her clothes. "How about now?"

"It seems to be working," he said after a moment or two.

"Yes, you are as good as new. Let me get a condom from my purse." She reached in and drew out a small gun.

"Hugo, you are a beautiful man. If we were only in a different business, but we make choices and life follows. Now we are *fini*." She fired one shot, hitting his heart. She tidied up and left his hands resting on his dick. On the way out, she took the keys to his van.

Chapter Twenty-One

"Which of you two gentlemen wanted to see me?" Detective O'Brien asked as he came down the stairs. He checked his watch—9:30 p.m.

"We both did," Sheppard answered as he and Billy Dee got up. He flashed his badge and introduced Billy Dee as a retired detective.

"What can I do for you?"

O'Brien stood a foot taller than each of them and about ten years younger than Sheppard and twenty for Billy Dee.

"I'm told you're talking to the wife of Joe Daniels. Her husband was a victim of a bomb that went off in the Palace parking lot yesterday afternoon."

"We got news on that. What time did it happen?"

"Around 1800 hours, give or take. You don't know?"

"We've been busy on homicides. That's what we do."

Sheppard patted himself looking for his cigarettes.

"Lose something?" O'Brien asked.

"Nah, must have left the smokes in the car. Let me get to the point, her husband was taken to Northwestern and now he's gone. We'd like to talk to her."

"We can't do anything for you at the moment. We have our own inquiry."

Sheppard straightened and looked directly at the detective. "Yeah, what's that about?"

"You're not part of this, so for now I can't tell you," O'Brien said.

"For your information, I am part of this. She's part of our investigation."

"Sorry, bud, you ain't go'n up there."

"Fuck off." Sheppard moved toward the stairs.

O'Brien blocked him.

"Move out of the damn way," Sheppard said.

Billy Dee took a step or two toward the two detectives. "This ain't go'n be good for nobody. So, everyone chill for a minute. Whatever you have, O'Brien, I'm sure it's important. We're not going to take your case. It's yours. All we want is to talk to her about her husband."

"Who are you again?" O'Brien asked. His shoulders relaxed.

"I worked here as the jail keeper. But before I retired I was promoted to detective."

"Huh?"

"I was rewarded."

"Don't be your usual modest son-of-a-bitch self," Sheppard broke in. He then turned to O'Brien. "Billy Dee solved that baseball player case Jack Rakow."

O'Brien scratched the top of his head. "I think I saw that on Facebook. I was on the West side at the time." He shrugged. "New game, new rules, nobody's talk'n to her until we're done." He put his hands on his hips. "If that's a problem, go see the commander."

"You're a real piece of work," Sheppard said.

"We can take it outside."

Sheppard retreated toward Billy Dee.

"Just what I thought." O'Brien looked Sheppard up and down and then went back up the stairs.

Chapter Twenty-Two

What the fuck? Joe Daniels blinked. *Sweat* dripped down his face as he pulled himself up into a sitting position. *This definitely isn't a hospital and I certainly am not in a hospital bed.* He heard voices coming from another room.

"Hey," he shouted, "Someone there?"

The voices stopped, and he caught the sound of footsteps. A female dressed in jeans and a work shirt stood at the doorway.

"He awake," she said.

Seconds later, a skinny short Black man joined her.

"If it ain't the great Joe Daniels enjoy'n our crib," he rolled out his laugh.

"What the… What is going on?" Daniels asked. "We can't be seen together. What are you doing, Bug?"

Bug took a few steps toward the couch. "I'd check yourself for roaches. Dat thing you ly'n on…"

"God damn it, Bug." Daniels brushed imagined or real cockroaches off his body.

"You look like a fool do'n dat." Bug knelt a foot or two from Daniels. "Dey like to get into your pubes and ass."

"What?" He went for his pants.

"What you do'n, Daniels, my woman be here."

Daniels looked up. He was breathing hard. "Okay, okay." He tried to stand but fell back onto the couch. "Help me up, Bug. What's the matter with you?"

Bug stood. "Was dat an order? Were you tell'n me to do something?"

Daniels shook his head. "No, man." His mouth was dry and it was difficult to speak. "I'm ask'n," his voice now a whisper.

"You hear dat, Nakisha. Joe Daniels be ask'n. Ain't dat a bitch?"

"Look, Bug, I'm not feeling well. If I pissed you off, I'm sorry, but Jesus man, some fuck'n bomb nearly blew me to bits. Whatever the problem, I'll straighten it out. Just get me to a doctor."

"Yeah, you gon'n to make good all right. Uhm hmm. Here the thing, Mr. Daniels, you know Drey be pissed. Dem boom sticks you got us were for shit." Bug moved within inches of him. "S-h-e-e-t, you hear? I tooks it upon myself to makes you understand the seriousness of de situation. I don't wants Drey comm'n after me and you don't either. He's de meanest sonofabitch I know, and patience ain't one of his virtues."

Daniels rubbed his face with his hands. What world was he in? *He was the boss man. Running guns got him clients and prestige with those that counted and money. Lots of goddamn money.* The room spun.

"He go'n zonked," Nakisha said.

Daniels felt something cold and wet strike his face. He wiped the water from his eyes. *What the hell?*

"He back, Nakisha, and not polite after you got that drink for him."

"Can I hit him?" she asked.

Bug laughed. "Girl, you time will come, but for now, I go'n to talk to my man so get to the bed and heat it up. This won't take long."

Daniels heard the click of her heels going down the hall and then a squeak of a door. Bug took a chair and swung it around. He sat and leaned over the top. "It taken you awhile to wake. S-h-e-e-t it be 2 in the morning. This is my time of day. You know what I'm say'n?" He turned his head and spat. " I've never seen you look so white, Daniels."

"You would be…never mind. I feel like shit." He squeezed his eyes shut, then re-opened them.

"Here de thing. Drey made a bad deal, you know what I'm talk'n. Those sticks dat were delivered couldn't shoot noth'n. My man got hit because the damn thing backfired. He in bad shape over at the County, and on top of dat caught a case. So, you go'n to work your magic for him."

Daniels nodded.

"Then you go'n to make de deal right. You gots a week. Den it be out of my hands."

Chapter Twenty-Three

Two months before that November evening when Joe didn't make it to Nicole's apartment, she was working at the law firm in her office. The clock radio on her desk read 7:00 p.m. Joe walked in.

"Thanks for staying late," he said.

"No problem." She swept a strand of hair from her face.

"That's what I like about you."

She smiled. "Is that the only thing?"

He didn't hesitate. "That sharp witty tongue of yours."

"I could say the same."

"A lawyer's best part."

She laughed, "Really?" And got up from her desk and came toward him.

"That's not bad, either." He grabbed her around the waist. "Actually, everything about you."

"Is that so." She loosened his tie, then ran a finger over his jaw line and then his mouth. Their eyes locked. She parted her lips. The kiss was hot and awakened her senses. She could feel it also awakened his.

He caught his breath, and then straightened his tie. "I took the liberty of ordering dinner," he said, trying to calm the situation.

"You did?"

He wore a cat-caught –the-canary smile. "Since we're going to work late. It's the least I can do."

"Uh-huh."

"Here?"

"No, someplace else. I've found sometimes the best work needs a different location to get the juices flowing." He paused, "Offices can confine... thinking."

"I see." She put a finger to her lips. "Where could dinner be that accomplishes that?"

He edged himself toward the doorway. "I've got a place at the Allerton. The room number is 2304. Leave fifteen minutes after me." His stare went through her. She saw his hand tremor. "And bring the Simon file."

"The Simon file? Of course. And dinner?"

"You won't believe what is being prepared."

"Sounds irresistible."

He walked out of her office. She sat back and put the tip of her pen to her lips. It hadn't taken long—from July-- two months. There was the innocent flirting. The embarrassed giggle when he made an off-color comment. She turned him down a few times, but always gave him hope. Men like Joe soldier on, thinking her capitulation was only a matter of time because of their power.

She gathered her things and went into Joe's office for the file. She rolled her eyes and searched his desk. There was a stack of law books and a pad with case citations. She lingered over it. *What the hell?* The Simon file was underneath. She pulled it out and stuffed it in her oversized leather bag. She waited for the time to pass and then went downstairs and caught a cab. What else will Simple Simon say?

***

"You know I'm married," Joe said, as she stood in the foyer.

"I sort of figured."

"I've cheated before, but I don't make a habit of it."

"Good to know."

"No really. I'm not one of those guys who plays around for the sake of playing around. It's just…"

"Joe, I'm not into confessions. We're two adults. And we are working late. Right?"

He undid his tie and shirt collar. "I just want you to know that I hired you on your merits. You had a hell of a resume. I, well, didn't expect this."

"Neither did I. Just for the record."

Chapter Twenty-Four

Detective Kerpnacki was at her desk typing a supple-mental report on the homicide of Anatoly Dmursic. She looked up when her partner O'Brien returned from downstairs.

"What was that about?" she asked.

"Noth'n. A shithead dick from Bomb and Arson wanted to horn in on our case. I told him to take a hike."

She smiled. "You do have a way with words."

"It's called **art**-tic-u-lation."

"Well, maybe you can articulate your way into this damn report."

He seemed to give it some thought by peering over her shoulder and reading. "You're doing great," he said, "I couldn't add a thing."

"Is that so?" She made a face.

"Did the medical examiner come back with cause of death?" he asked.

She looked at her watch. "No, but it had to be gun- shot wounds. Hell, we have the weapon and our defendant all but admitted it was hers."

"Is that what your notes say?"

She grabbed her papers and used her finger to run down the page. She then looked up. "Didn't the Beretta come back to her?"

O'Brien had wandered across the room to grab a cup of coffee. "What was that?" he asked.

"The gun. Wasn't it registered to Beth Daniels?"

He set the coffee on the desk and rummaged through another stack of documents. "Found it."

"Well?"

"Beth definitely had an FOID card."

"We know that."

"Hold on." He flipped some more pages. "Shit." He dropped the hard copy of the e-mail response from the Illinois State Police. "The damn thing comes back to Dmursic."

"What? Let me see." She grabbed the paper and studied it. "Did you know this when we talked to Beth?"

"Come on, Kerpnacki, that's not what I do. This must have come in after we locked her up. Besides, it doesn't rule her out."

She gave him a hard look. "It's no longer a slam dunk. Hope her fingerprints are all over the gun." She sighed and stepped away from her computer. "What did Bomb and Arson want with Beth?"

"Huh? Oh, the dick said Daniels' husband was missing after he went to the hospital."

"Well, if this is a love triangle between Anatoly, Daniels, and her, maybe little Ms. Beth was even busier than we thought."

"You think?"

Chapter Twenty-Five

Paris

Monsieur Dumond arrived a half-hour early at the Hotel Duquesne Eiffel. He scouted the lobby, which had few people even for November and then went to Reception. The woman behind the desk appeared to concentrate on a piece of paper. Dumond saw the writing was handwritten. She looked up while she turned the note on its blank side.

"*Bonne après midi,*" she recovered, "how may I help you?"

She seemed to be in her mid-twenties. Her skin was olive and her hair black and curly. Her French was excellent but he couldn't place the accent.

"I'm to meet a friend." He checked his watch. "I'm a little early."

"Are you or your friend visiting with us?"

He smiled. "We are to have lunch."

"Oh, in that case the restaurant is on the second floor. But should you decide to stay we have rooms with wonderful views of Paris."

"*Merci,*" he said, "you've been most kind. I have a life-long hobby of placing people by their accent. Where did you learn French?"

"You must be mistaken. I am French."

He gave her a hard look and after a slight pause said, "Yes, of course. I misspoke."

Her tone hardened. "*Bon appetit.*"

He thanked her again and took the staircase to the second floor. The maître d' showed him to a window table. He pulled out the chair.

"I'd rather sit facing the entrance. Thank you."

"But Monsieur, you are missing the view."

He shrugged. "I'm waiting for a friend."

The maître de gave a knowing smile. "*Bien,*" and walked away.

Dumond took in the room. The walls were painted light blue edged with royal blue. The vaulted ceiling had gold specks that were peeling. The tables were adorned with linen and separated to provide privacy. Yes, a tourist would believe this is how the French dine. The staff glided noiselessly over the heavy carpet. He checked the time. It was slightly past one.

There were several tables of couples and many empty ones. No one seemed to be waiting except him.

"Would you like to order a refreshment? Some wine or perhaps a cocktail?" A waiter interrupted.

Dumond glanced at the menu. "Your 1992 Marc de Bourgogne, please."

"*Oui,*" and the server disappeared.

Dumond sipped water from the crystal glass while he waited. When he was younger, he trained himself to have patience. It was an invaluable tool. But age had made time precious. It was now seven minutes after one. Not unreasonable, but the son of a bitch was late. He checked his phone for messages. There was one from Susan, but before he read it, he sensed a change and looked up. A woman stood in the entranceway not far from the maître d's podium. She wore a leather jacket and leather pants. He tried not to stare but there was something familiar about her. Same hair and build but no hotel blazer; it was the receptionist.

He saw her scan the room. The maître d' took a few steps toward her. She said something to him and then entered the dining room. She looked again and then came toward Dumond. She smiled.

He put his hand in his jacket pocket and felt his pistol. As she got closer, he started to rise. "To what do I owe—"

He focused on her face and only noticed what her sleeve covered at the last second.

"For Hugo." She fired and walked past.

His shirt turned red. *Hugo?* His knees buckled and he fell. His thoughts were jumbled. He didn't understand. The pain built and his breathing grew labored. The last thing remembered was her accent. She was not from Paris.

Chapter Twenty-Six

Chicago

Susan didn't understand why Dumond had not responded to her text message. She was sure he was up. It was around one p.m. Paris time and even a Frenchman didn't sleep past noon. She eyed the clock near her bed. It was so damn early and dark. It had been a restless sleepless night. The picture of Hugo lying naked and shot wouldn't leave her. She ran through her list that justified his killing. He was a pig. He shouldn't have attacked her. But the thought that she may have overreacted made her anxious. Hell, she'd got the weapons without paying. The deal became more profitable. Dumond would certainly see it that way. Okay, there was the small problem of getting those things from here to there, but certainly Dumond would know. Ten minutes passed, and still no response. She scooched up in bed and turned on the lamp on the nightstand. She checked her phone again. Nothing. Sleep was no longer possible. Instead, she took a quick shower and put on some old jeans and a sweater. She threw on a jacket that hung on the back of a chair and decided to start the morning at Starbucks. She stuck her hand in the pocket. *Shit, keys.* She threw the coat off and then picked it up off the floor. It was the same one she'd worn when Hugo was shot. She stared at her hand and sank into a chair. After the shooting, she drove the van to a storage locker rented a week earlier. It was late at night and the place was empty. She put the hood of her coat over her face and unloaded the crates. It was the best she could do to hide from the cameras. When she finished, she hopped back into the van and left it in the back of Hugo's warehouse. By the time she finally got home, she was exhausted and had forgotten about his keys. *So stupid of her.*

She looked toward the front door. The only sound was the usual morning noise of people on their way to work or school. She went to the window overlooking the street and peeked through the blinds from her second-floor view. She held her breath. There seemed to be no strange cars or trucks parked. She looked away and allowed herself to exhale. She rubbed her face. Her hands were cold and felt numb. Fear exaggerated her thoughts and it wasn't even seven. She had to talk to Dumond. He would know what to do. He always did. *Why the fuck is he not answering?*

Her phone burst the oppressive quiet by playing *La Marseillaise*. She jumped. Someone was calling. She had to push the slide on the phone two to three times in order to answer.

"*Allo, bon*, hello," she said, "*allo*, Dumond?"

"Hello," said a deep-sounding male voice, "I have a message from Google business. Your profile—"

"What?" She whipped the phone from her ear and looked at the number. She didn't know anyone from Texas. She pounded the End button several times with her thumb and yelled at her phone. Her hand trembled and it fell out of her palm, hitting the floor. She didn't move. Maybe this was a sign. Had Dumond abandoned her? Had he changed plans without telling her? She'd survived before she'd met him, and she would do so again. The overriding question was why?

Chapter Twenty-Seven

Bug had Joe Daniels bundled into a van and dumped in the west Loop. It was late enough that there were few people around when Daniels landed on the pavement. Daniels looked up and saw the driver stick his hand that gripped his cell outside the van 's window.

"Hey, don't do that. Please…"

The driver gave Daniels a look. He let Daniels come within twenty feet and then dropped it. Daniels saw the driver's smile reflected in the side mirror as he gunned the engine and roared off.

"Son of a bitch," Daniels said as he hobbled toward the phone. "Jesus, I hope it works." He picked it up. The case must have protected it, as there were no cracks. His fingers labored to punch in Beth's phone number. It was damn cold outside and all he had on was a long-sleeve shirt. *Bug could have at least given him a jacket. Damn him.* He held the phone to his ear but no one answered. He looked at his wrist but his iWatch wasn't there. He hung up and saw the time on his phone. *Where the hell could my trampy wife be at three in the morning? My world is falling apart. Who else could I call?* The cold was getting to him. Chicago's winds cut through the thin cloth of his shirt. His teeth chattered. He had to get to some place warm. He thought of a cab. He grabbed for his wallet. The credit cards were gone and there was only a $1 bill. *Shit.* He looked up and down the street. There were no other crazy fools out in this weather.

Nicole. He'd call her. He couldn't think of anything else. The irony hit him as he punched her number. She was the last nice thought he'd had before the explosion … was it only last evening? *My God I can't remember.*

"Hello?"

The voice was breathy, and for a moment Daniels had forgotten he dialed.

"Yes, hello, thank God, Nicole, can you come get me?"

"What? Get you…where? Is this Joe?"

"Yes, yes, it's Joe."

Sleep went out of her voice. "Joe. I've been so worried. Where have you been? The office tried the hospital and couldn't get information, and the secretary called your wife and couldn't reach her. Joe, what is going on? Where are you?"

He looked around for a street sign or a familiar sight, while he pressed the phone to his ear. "I'll explain everything but right now…I'm not…sure. I'm going to look." He dragged himself to a corner. "I'm someplace on…" An El train rumbled above him. "Can you hear me? Nicole, hold on…"

A gust of wind caught him. His fingers numb from the cold caused him to drop his cell. He floundered through his frozen tears to find it.

"Nicole," he shouted, "Nichole, don't hang up?"

He fell to the ground, his hands searching. *Where the hell is it?* He slowly brought himself into a kneeling position. Pain shot up his legs. He had to stand. He reached for some kind of support. He felt a pressure on his shoulder.

"Hey, man, what you doin'?"

He turned as best he could and saw a bearded man dressed in a hooded patched parka.

"My phone," he said.

"No man, what the fuck you do'n with no coat. This ain't beach weather.

Daniels had no answer. "I need to find my phone," he said ignoring the question.

"You mean this piece of shit?" The parka man held it out in front of him. "How much you go'n to give me for it?"

He couldn't tell if that was his phone. "I… I… Look as soon as my friend picks me up you'll get whatever you want."

"S-h-i-t you lost your mind. I'll just keep it." He took a step or two away.

Daniels was on all fours blindly searching.

"You a sight. Here. I don't know what I do with it anyways. Can't drink it. Fuck you all." He dropped it and walked away.

Daniels crawled to the spot. His hand trembled as he picked it up. "Hello, Nicole… please… are you there?"

Chapter Twenty-Eight

"I was this close to punching the smirk off O'Brien's face." Sheppard indicated a quarter inch between his thumb and forefinger. "The punk son of a bitch, maybe that's what we should do is go to the commander."

Billy Dee ushered his partner out the door of the police station and to the parking lot. "Don't think that's a good idea."

"Why the fuck not?"

"Whose side do you think the *white shirt* will be on. The guy who works for him or an outsider…you."

Sheppard was about to answer but changed his mind; instead, he told Billy Dee to get in the vehicle. He started the engine and backed out. "I'm calling it a night. I'll drive you back to your car. I don't want to get on your wife's bad side."

"I appreciate that. I don't either."

Night traffic was light and it didn't take long to get to Roosevelt Road.

"Hey, by tomorrow morning maybe Daniel's wife will be able to talk or Mr. Daniels will show up. Things happen."

Sheppard frowned. "Yeah and the tooth fairy will leave money under the pillow. Anyway, thanks for tagging along."

"No problem, Shep. It felt good doing police work." Billy Dee got into his Chrysler 200 and drove off.

***

Billy Dee knew from having worked years in lockup that at some point the homicide dicks would put Beth Daniels in a cell if she were going to be charged. It was more of a question of when and not if. He still had clout in the jailer department, as he was tight with the man who replaced him. He checked the time—way past midnight. He was in deep shit with the wife. He pulled his car over and checked his phone. *Jesus I am in trouble.* He punched in his home number, but then thought better. *Text messaging was invented for this purpose.*

"Janine, sorry babe, I've been helping Shep on a case, and had my phone off. Everything is ok. I'll talk to you when I can."

He knew all he did was put off her tirade for later. *After all these years, she should be used to it. But ever since that baseball player's case, she hasn't been the same.*

He went for his half-smoked cigar left in the ashtray and lit it. After a few puffs, it was as good as new. *At least in my car I am king.* He eyed his phone. His wife must be asleep. She hadn't called. He chomped down on the stogie. *Time to call in a favor.* He phoned O.B., the man who'd replaced him as jailer.

"Lockup, Area North, Bently."

"Is that you, O.B.?"

"Who this?"

"Come on, man, you forget already?"

There was a moment's pause.

"I'll be damned, Billy Dee?"

"Sure is."

"Haven't heard from you in a long time. What you up to?"

"Whatever the wife say, you know how that goes."

"I hear you, man." O.B. laughed. "So, what the hell you do'in call'n at this hour?"

"You remember Detective Sheppard from Bomb and Arson?"

"B and A, don't get many from them."

"Don't matter. He be work'n on that explosion at the Palace parking lot."

"Yeah, I heard about that. Capt'n say glad it isn't his baby. You know all the heat from the Hall."

"Uh huh, here's what I'm ask'n. You have a female in the lockup. The name is Beth Daniels. Homicide is holding her."

"Female? You sure homicide? Most are hookers from Boystown or North Avenue."

"Can you check?"

"No problem."

Billy Dee heard the phone smack probably the top of O.B.'s desk. In the past, the list of detainees would be on sheets of paper. Now everything was computerized. He had a feeling O.B. still did it the old way.

"I gots the list. What her name? Spell it."

"D-a-n."

"Dan?" O.B asked.

"No, Daniels, Beth."

"Let me see."

Billy Dee heard his friend mumble down the list.

"Ashoff, Brodie, D-a, here go Daniels, Beth."

"Damn, O.B., you did good. You don't mind if I drive over."

"Mind? What for?"

"Need to talk to her. It has to do with the Palace."

"Let me think on it."

"O.B., it's a favor."

"Yeah, I know, but you ain't police anymore."

"O.B. I'll call you when I'm in the back. Just open the door and tell me the cell. Nobody has to know."

"I don't know, Billy Dee."

"It's important."

"Okay, but no fuckups."

"You got it."

Chapter Twenty-Nine

"The captain been nosing around up here while you were putting Beth Daniels to bed in the lockup," O'Brien said. "Did you say anything to him?"

"Hell no. Why?" Kerpnacki asked.

"'Cause he asked to see us when you came back."

She wasn't sure O'Brien believed her. "Look, I'm your partner. My name is on the report just like yours. I think Daniels killed Dmursic, whether with her gun or his."

He held his hand up. "Hey, you had me at 'hell'." He picked up the file. "Let's see what the boss wants."

They took the stairs to the first floor and stepped into the outer office. The captain was at his desk with a phone to his ear. He motioned them in.

The captain put his hand over the receiver. "You guys know a fella, goes by the name Hugo. He has a warehouse around Fulton Street."

"Hugo? Any last name?" O'Brien asked.

The captain held up a finger to wait and returned to his phone conversation. "Where's that restaurant?" He asked. "Oh, Huron?" He scribbled an address on his notepad, laughed and hung-up. "A dinner meeting," he explained and then his smile vanished.

"What's the name of the victim on your homicide case?"

O'Brien opened his folder. He ran his finger down the page. "Dmursic, Anatoly," he said.

"What nationality?"

Kerpnacki gave O'Brien a look. "I don't know, Polish? Maybe Russian?"

"Did you search his place?" the captain asked.

O'Brien shifted in his seat. "Well, by the time we got there, the beat guys and ETs were wrapping up. They gave us their notes, and we went to interview potential witnesses."

"So, you didn't search yourselves."

"Other than checking out the body, not a hell of lot. I told Kerpnacki to look in the bedroom."

"Find anything?" the captain asked.

Kerpnacki stole a glance at O'Brien. She placed her hands on the chair's armrest. "No sir. There was the usual stuff. Nothing of much interest."

The captain picked up a pen and doodled. "Nothing much, huh," he said without looking up.

Kerpnacki squirmed in her seat. "Was there something I missed?"

"I don't know. Was there?" he said.

She stared straight ahead and waited.

The captain looked up after several seconds. "You guys hear of the SLA?"

Kerpnacki glanced at O'Brien, then said, "No."

"You?" The captain turned to O'Brien.

"SLA? Weren't they a hippie/ antigovernment group back in the seventies? Sym-some such shit liberation army."

"Nice—but no." He leaned down and grabbed a bag and poured the contents on the desk. "These papers and things were found in Dmursic's safe."

"Safe?" Kerpnacki bit her lip.

"Yeah. A beat officer, let me see," the captain searched his desk. "Here it is." He read from a scrap of paper. "His name is Kusic. He went back and found it built into a sox drawer. The ET boys got it opened."

Kerpnacki leaned closer and tried to read them. After staring at it, she looked up. "It's not in English."

"Good, detective. What language is it?"

"I don't know, sir."

"You want to take a crack at it, O'Brien?"

O'Brien didn't move. "English is all I got. Never bothered with another."

The captain took the papers. "It's Serbian. SLA stands for the Serbian Liberation Army. According to what Dmursic wrote, this fellow Hugo is part of this organization and into running guns. There's another name that pops up." He pointed midway down the sheet. "Nicole, and then over here 'Daniels'. That's your offender, yes?"

"Yeah, Beth Daniels," the detectives said in unison.

Chapter Thirty

Nicole held the phone to her ear. "Hello? Joe?" She heard a high pitch metal on metal squeal. The noise was so sharp she pulled the cell away. "Damn." She glared at it and at the same time, shouted Joe's name. Air whistled through the receiver and then nothing. She looked at the face of the mobile and saw the talk minutes continue.

"Hello, hello, Joe?" In desperation, she hit the end button, and then redialed. No connection. She dialed again. The call didn't go through. She gripped the phone and looked at the time—3:10 a.m. *What the fuck is going on?*

A feeling like one gets riding a roller coaster caused her to cradle her stomach. She laid there for a few seconds, then turned on the table lamp and readjusted the pillows. *Was Joe at a hospital? On the street? What about Beth, his wife? Why didn't he call her?* She tried to recreate the last few minutes. Joe's voice was strained, almost scared. *Scared of what or who?* She punched in the number again. The line was dead. She fell back on her pillows. *Maybe her scheme was becoming too complicated.* She was well versed in handling men and the bedroom, but why get involved with guns. Anatoly and she would have done fine had they kept it simple. She sighed and closed her eyes for a second or two.

What a night. Well, if I'm up, I shouldn't have to suffer alone. She opened the drawer of her nightstand and found her other phone. She dialed… Anatoly. There was no answer. *Shit, what is everyone doing at this hour?* When she'd talked to him last evening, he had told her there was someone at the door. *Was it Beth? That didn't make sense. She had to know that Joe was injured and taken to a hospital. It was all over the fuck'n news. Was he working another scam? If he was, he had stamina.* She hesitated to leave a message, but her worries overcame her caution. "Call," she said, and pushed end.

She got out of bed and went to the back of her closet. There was a small floor safe buried behind shoeboxes and clothes. She swept the pile with her hand and knelt in front of the dial. The closet light was dim. She fumbled for the flashlight app on her phone. *Where the hell is it?* After several seconds, she found the symbol and the light lit the screen. She spun the combination and the door opened. She separated the various papers, cash, tax returns, and bankbooks until she found a copy of the Simon folder. The same file Joe had asked her to bring the first time she went to his *pied-à-terre* at the Allerton. She got up, brushed a strand of hair from her face, and went back to her bed. She sat cross-legged and emptied the folder on her lap. *Could this be the cause?* She thought back to that night at the Allerton.

***

It was an evening to remember even for her. Joe was true to his word. There was dinner, wine, and they did work late.

The cab ride from the office to his place took ten minutes. The hotel had been renovated. It was now sleek and modern. She walked through the entrance, passed reception, and took the elevator to the twenty-third floor. The hallway was long and heavily carpeted with fixtures like candles lighting the way. His suite was at the other end. She knocked once, found the door open, and stepped in. Joe came from the living room. She was still in the foyer when he gave that confessional about cheating. He was so sincere and a touch vulnerable. He wrapped his arms around her, touching her back lightly. Their lips met and that kiss did more than any cup of coffee.

"Happy you're glad to see me," she said catching her breath.

He smiled and kissed her again. When he let her go, he said, "I've been waiting for this for a while."

"Me too."

He took her coat. "Did you bring that file?"

"It's in my purse. Is this what we will be working on?" She opened her case and handed it to him.

"Of course," he said, and then asked, "red or white. I prefer red—much more flavor and full bodied."

"Wine is wine."

He gave her a hurt look. "You can't mean that?"

"Well… what I meant was after a few glasses…"

He shrugged and walked to the kitchen with the file.

He came back with two beautiful glasses filled halfway, the liquid the color of a blazing sunset.

"To us and tonight," he said.

They clinked.

"Now, swirl the wine, then take a small sip."

She tilted the glass and let the liquid touch her tongue. Seconds passed. "Well?" he asked.

"Wow, there's all these flavors."

"See."

He took a sip and then put the glass down on a table. He took her hand and led her to the bedroom. The room had soft light and the silhouetted illumination of the city's skyscrapers shone through the windows.

He undressed her in a gentle manner, kissing her bare skin as her clothing fell to the floor. The covers of the bed had already been pulled back so that she felt the silken sheets underneath. She had to admit that she could get used to this treatment.

He sat on the side of the bed and gazed at her. "You are beautiful, you know."

Compliments like that usually had little meaning. After all, most of the time men said it to get her into bed. But it sounded as if he meant it. She felt her face flush. "Thanks," and tried to reach for him.

He took her hand and put it aside. He leaned over and put his mouth on her breast, and then his hand slid down her body. She was more than ready. That time it may have been short but God almighty it was sweet. Between their lovemaking, they ate and finished two or three bottles of wine. They were exhausted and satiated when dawn peeked through their windows. She opened her eyes and found Joe asleep on the edge of the king size bed. She slipped away, first stopping at the bathroom. She washed her face and stepped into the kitchen. The file she had brought was in his opened briefcase. No noise came from the bedroom. *What the hell?* She leaned down and opened it. There was a copy of a lawsuit, motions, and more paper. *Nothing unusual.* She sifted through the pages until she came to some handwritten notes.

"Bug 12 sticks, 100 caps, 14 gats, 25k. Drey."

What the fuck? She looked up from the notes. *Was Joe stirring?* She dropped the file back in his case and went back to bed.

***

She stared at the copied note held in her hand. "Bug? Drey? Who or is it what?" She picked up her cell again and dialed Joe's number. It rang.

"Joe?"

Chapter Thirty-One

She'll leave. *Why not?* Dumond had sent her to Chicago, and now he had abandoned her. *Il devrait se baiser lui-même*, he should go fuck himself. How could he have done that? Susan did everything he asked. Why would he be pissed at her? Her anger mounted. A new woman? Someone younger, or maybe older who of course had money. He'd play her for every euro, franc, or dollar. *Quel putain*, what the fuck? She yanked at the bureau drawer in the living room. Behind receipts and papers was a wad of cash. She grabbed it. This was her safety money—about $400.00. She stuffed the bills in her jacket pocket and strode to the hallway. She had one hand on the doorknob; the other gripped the stash. She glanced back and saw the imprint of her heels on the rug. *Shit. Where would I go? The money wouldn't take me far and credit cards were useless. Plastic was traceable.* She learned that lesson from Dumond. She recited his words: *"Cash is freedom. It opens doors, shuts eyes, and closes mouths."* He was wise. An unintended smile crept over her lips. It made her think. She took her jacket off and put the money back in its hiding place.

There could be another explanation. Perhaps his meeting with the client was called off or the *flics* got too close. The police were always watching him. That's what made him… Dumond. He carried out his feats in front of their eyes. She sighed. She would try him later.

She plopped down on the couch with her feet curled

underneath. *What to do?* She wrapped her arms around herself and rocked. *I have to get rid of Hugo's keys.* She sat up. *What else could tie me to him?* She had wiped most of the surfaces in his apartment and didn't see anyone when she left. She suspected she was not the first woman to leave his apartment in the morning. *Who's to say what is known and who knows it?* She was just another twenty-something woman with looks and smarts, more of a beddable type than a killer. Those characteristics had gotten her through other scrapes. There was no reason to doubt they wouldn't succeed this time. She stretched her legs and began to feel better. Then she caught her breath. If something happened to Dumond… If he was…. She had been his lover, and he, her teacher. His enduring lesson was: take what was given. Adaptation meant survival. She mulled those thoughts. She eyed Hugo's keys. It occurred to her, that link to the late arms seller could lead to an opportunity. Hugo had customers. She had guns. The possibilities brought a smile. Her left palm began to itch—a wives' tale that meant money was coming.

Chapter Thirty-Two

Billy Dee parked in the rear of the police station near the prisoner loading dock it was closing in on 2 a.m. He imagined O.B., the jail-keeper, wringing his hands and cussing to himself. Something he always did when his nerves got to him. Hopefully after all the mutterings, O.B. would unlock the door. Billy Dee cut the engine and unhooked his seat belt. His hand was on the door handle when a beam of light hit the dock. In the doorway stood O.B. with two others—a male and a female. *Shit what has he gone and done. That boy either thinks too much or not at all.* O.B.'s hands were moving and he could tell O.B. was upset. He watched and realized there was a third person—another female who was handcuffed. He leaned forward to get a better look. *I'll be damned.* The male standing closer to O.B. was the detective with whom he and Shep had their disagreement—O'Brien. *What the hell was going on?* He didn't dare roll his window down. Even if it meant he couldn't hear. So far, he hadn't been noticed. He watched the argument for another minute or two. It ended with O'Brien, the handcuffed woman, and the other female crossing the dock toward the stairs that led to the parking lot on the other side of the building. He heard O.B. shout and then slam the back door. He was sure O.B. would be grabbing the nearest phone and raising hell with the captain. He cracked his window and listened. A car engine started. He had a hunch the prisoner was Beth Daniels and O'Brien with his partner were going back to the scene of the homicide.

He had no business or authority to follow. He was retired—no more cops and robbers. What he should do is call Shep. *It's his case, his mess.* This had nothing to do with him anymore. *Man, Janine ever knew.* He shook his head and smiled to himself. He then looked at the time—*no way.* It was well past Shep's bedtime as well as his. *So, I'll play cop a little while longer. What the hell, I'm the one who's up.*

It had been awhile since Billy Dee shadowed a subject. What was taught at the academy was one thing, but the real deal another. He popped the cigar in his mouth and lit it. If he's going for a ride, he might as well get some enjoyment. He backed his car out and swung around the police building. He could see O'Brien's vehicle ahead at the intersection making a right onto Western. At least he's got surprise on his side.

Traffic was sparse and he tried to keep a good distance. They went south until Diversey and then hopped on the expressway toward downtown. *Where the hell are they going? Back to Daniels' apartment? Why?* They passed Ohio Street, which would have been the exit, but O'Brien kept going until Randolph. There he got off the highway and at the intersection made a right to go west. *What the hell?* At Morgan, they turned north toward Lake Street. Billy Dee saw a bum on the sidewalk as he made the turn. *Jesus, poor guy. He didn't even have a winter coat.* There was an instant where he thought of stopping, but he'd lose O'Brien. They were going west on Lake again. The Elevated train was above. What was once a heavy industrial area, populated by prostitutes and down-and-outs, was being transformed into condos and expensive restaurants. The area though still had a ways to go. A block ahead, O'Brien made a left. As Billy Dee pulled to the intersection, he saw the detective stop in front of a warehouse driveway. He had no choice but to drive past. He turned to catch the sign above the door—*Hugo's Fresh Fruit Market.*

Chapter Thirty-Three

Joe stared at the phone and prayed it still worked. He gingerly held it to his ear and heard a voice. "Nicole, thank God," he said and closed his eyes for a second.

"Joe?"

"It's me, it's me." He took a breath. "I'm at... Jesus, please... get over here."

"What? I don't understand. Where are you? What's going on?"

He looked around to see if anyone else was near. He had to become coherent. "I know, I know—crazy—just come. I'll explain... everything."

"Come? Where? Are you hurt? Where's your wife?"

He saw lights of a car coming toward him. He moved as best he could to hide in a doorway. "Nicole, I don't ..." He swallowed hard. "Baby...I'm so...cold."

"Freezing? What happened to your coat? You're scaring me."

He bent over to shield himself from the wind. "Sorry, I'm so sorry. Everything will be okay." His breath blew into the phone.

"Joe?"

He gathered his strength. "Nicole, get into your car... drive here. For God's sake—fast."

"I'm not even dressed. I'm in bed. It's what..." She stole a look at her clock. "It's 2:30 in the fuck'n morning."

What am I doing? Get out of the fuck'n bed. "You've been awake at this hour before," he said instead.

She paused, "Yeah, but I was doing something better."

"We both were. Please, Nicole, it's been…" He looked at the street sign. "I'm at Morgan and Lake Street."

"How? Never mind. It'll take me a few minutes to get dressed. You're not in the greatest area."

"Yeah… I know."

"It will be about twenty minutes."

"As soon as you can."

***

Nicole gathered the papers, including the Drey note, and returned them to the duplicate file. *What a girl has to do. This is above and beyond anything I had plotted in my scheme. If there were a next time, I'd keep it simple. Should I try Anatoly one more time? Ach. If he didn't pick up at 2:30, it's not likely he'll answer now. We will have a talk sometime tomorrow.*

She decided to throw on a pair of jeans and a sweatshirt. At this hour it wouldn't matter how she looked. However, she couldn't leave without brushing her hair and teeth. *Some things can't be skimped.* Ten minutes had gone by since she'd spoken to Joe. *If he has to wait, so be it. This is a favor and I expect to be rewarded.* She slammed her apartment door and took the elevator to the garage. She hated walking in a parking lot—alone. At this hour, only someone up to no good would be lurking. Her heels tapped on the cement and echoed through the garage. She stopped after a few steps and listened. There were no other sounds but hers. She peered down the row of vehicles, ready to hit the emergency button on her fob. Her car was at the end, about fifty yards away. Somewhere in the rows of parked cars, she heard the low rumble of an engine. She peered over her shoulder. There was nothing to see. She quickened her pace all the while listening. The palm of her hand grew clammy. Her car was twenty yards away. She looked back again.

A SUV lumbered down her aisle. Its lights were off. As the vehicle neared, it picked up speed. She was too shocked to scream. She tried to jump to the side but wasn't quick enough. The passenger door swung open and struck her. She fell on the back of another car and dropped the fob. Hands grabbed her and then a cloth covered her face.

Chapter Thirty-Four

Susan doused her flashlight when she heard noise. She had let herself into Hugo's warehouse by the back door. Now, she couldn't remember whether she'd relocked it. *It's always the obvious that fucks one up.* She strained to listen. There were voices by the side of the building. At least two that she could tell—a male and female. *Were they cops or potential arms customers? A woman buying guns? It didn't make sense. A woman?* She stopped. What the hell was she doing? Then, she thought, Hugo sold fruit and vegetables as his front. It could be deliveries. She drew her sleeve carefully and peeked at her watch. *It's too early for legitimate business. It has to be cops. Hugo's body has been discovered and here they are. Shit.* The voices went up the driveway and away from the back. *That door I was sure was locked.* She took a few steps and nearly tripped over something. The noise of things falling was like an explosion. She took a deep breath and stood very still. The front door rattled and shook. Then the voices came back down the side. She saw lights flicker on the outside of the building and she immediately ducked. Her heart raced. She was in a marathon. Thank God, Hugo had covered the windows with blinds. She heard the backdoor shake.

Someone asked if they had the key. A female said, "No."

"How the hell do you expect us to get in there?" The voice was male.

"Break it down," came an answer.

"We have no warrant. The captain would love that."

"You asked. Maybe Beth knows the way."

The voices sounded together. Someone tried the back door again, and then lights went up the driveway. She heard a door open and then an engine start.

She slowly got up. Sweat stuck her shirt to her body. She waited a few minutes, and then clicked on her flashlight.

Hugo's office was a mess. She saw the carton she had tripped over. Ledgers and files were all around. She knelt. On a sheet of notebook paper, there were three names: Anatoly, Nicole, and an arrow pointing to "J". After that were notations of amounts and then a dollar sign. *Was this for vegetables or guns?* She pocketed the sheet and then went through his desk. There was a bound notebook. She flipped the pages. *Wow.* She was in business.

Chapter Thirty-Five

Billy Dee drove down the block made a U and parked a good 200 feet across from Hugo's warehouse. He turned the car off and cracked the window a bit to keep them from fogging.

He could see O'Brien and his partner walk up the warehouse driveway. They came back and pulled the prisoner from their car. All three went to the front door. O'Brien was in the prisoner's face, his voice loud enough to be heard over the rumble of the El train. His partner acted a bit calmer. Whatever he was yelling about ended within minutes. He pushed the prisoner to the rear door of his vehicle, yanked it open and shoved her inside. The two officers argued. O'Brien walked away and jumped into the driver's seat. His partner scrambled to the other side and barely got in before O'Brien backed up. Tires squealed as the car raced down the street and away from Billy Dee.

He turned the ignition key and slowly moved toward the driveway. O'Brien was already a block away. The thought of following him faded as quickly as O'Brien's taillights. It was late—very late. He stopped, put the car in neutral, and grabbed the clipboard that rested on the passenger seat. He wrote down the address and name of where he was. He had no idea what'd led O'Brien here. *That's something for Shep to figure out.* The tension of the night dissipated, the adrenaline replaced by fatigue. He lit a new cigar and tried to put the pieces of the evening's work together.

A slight movement from the front of Hugo's caught his attention. He swore to himself the front door opened. *Ain't dat a bitch after all of O'Brien's pounding and shaking.* He stared but nothing else happened. *Maybe my eyes are playing tricks. Jesus what I'd give for a pair of binoculars.* Billy Dee put the cigar in the ashtray. When he looked again, the door opened a little wider. A silhouette stood in the doorway. Then disappeared inside the building. *Is that Hugo? Should I get out?* Just in case, he reached under his seat and grabbed his old police issued pistol—an old Colt revolver. It never jammed and it was accurate, unlike the newfangled semiautomatics. He put the gun on the passenger seat.

Without turning on his lights, he put the car in reverse and rolled back a few hundred feet. *Whoever that is don't work there.* He scanned the street for another parked vehicle. He looked behind him. *Where the fuck is the car?*

Seconds later, a small vehicle shot down the driveway and flew past him in the other direction. It was gone before he could react. The only thing he caught was the first letter of the license plate: S. He couldn't even identify the model except for its size. *What a great detective I am. Son-of-a-bitch.* He put his car in drive and drifted slowly toward Hugo's driveway. *Might as well have a look-see.*

He holstered his gun and got out. It felt good to stand and breathe the cold air. He used the flashlight app on his iPhone. There was a garage in the back. He shined the light through its window. Three stalls, but a van was parked outside. He tried the doors of the vehicle and garage but they were locked. *This is gett'n to be a waste of time.*

He moved toward the warehouse. *Son-of-a-gun.* The knob turned and the door opened with a slight push. Billy Dee's hand rested on his gun as he stepped inside. There were crates of fruits and vegetables everywhere. Some were stacked, others half open. *Must be a feast for the mice and rats.*

He moved cautiously, half crouched. After a few steps, he stopped to listen. If there was another son-of-a-bitch there, he wanted to be ready. He felt sweat trickle down his face. His back ached. *Damn. I'm too old for this. What was I thinking?* Time does funny things in these situations. He'd swear it took fifteen minutes to get from the warehouse to the office. But upon reflection it was more like two or three at the most. He straightened when he got there. He momentarily put the gun down to rub the kink from his lower back. It didn't help.

He picked up his weapon and stepped over an empty box. A pole lamp stood nearby. He flicked it on. Papers and ledgers flowed from the desk, a corner table, and the floor. *Either this Hugo keeps one hell of a fucked-up office or someone has been in here reorganizing.* He randomly picked up notebooks but couldn't make sense of what was written. The words, or maybe they were names, had weird letters, after which was a column of numbers. *Who is this guy?* He looked again. He had seen this alphabet before. Where? He took a breath while he eyed the room. He brushed his face with his gun hand as he tried to remember. He looked again at the paper. Russian? *They have that crazy ass alphabet. Yep, I seen this shit on the news. Holy Jesus, this Hugo maybe is some Russian Mafia guy into something besides fruit.* He thought of taking one of the books to show Shep but decided not to.

It was after three in the morning. It was time to leave. He'd come back during the day and hopefully meet the silhouette that was Hugo. In any case, something was beginning to stink and it wasn't the fruit. He shut the light and retreated to the warehouse. Near the back door was an opened case of apples. *What the hell?* Golden Delicious, his favorite. He holstered his gun and stooped down. He grabbed one, then hesitated and took another. For Janine, he thought, and put the apples in his coat pocket. The light from outside caught something near the door. It was a business card. The front read "Allied Storage." He bent down and picked it up. He turned the back of it and saw a written number, "2475 D." *What the hell is that about?* He stared at the card for a second or two, then decided to put it in his pocket. *Never know where this could lead.*

Chapter Thirty-Six

The captain glared at O'Brien and Kerpnacki. "Okay, you two idiots, explain what the fuck happened? Who told you to drag a prisoner…" He looked down at some paperwork. "What the hell was her…"

"Daniels, Beth, sir," Kerpnacki volunteered.

The captain looked up and glared. "Yeah, this Daniels woman."

There was silence.

"Anyone want to give me a goddamn answer? How about you, O'Brien?" Before he could speak, the Captain went on. "It better be good. Do you know who your so-called prisoner is married to? I'll tell you—Joe Daniels. And do either one of you dumb fucks know who that is? Of course you do. You're not completely stupid. You do read the papers once in a while."

"Yes, sir, we know all of that," Kerpnacki said.

"Great." The captain stood up, leaned forward, his palms flat on the desk. "Okay, here's something you don't know. Guess who turned up dead."

The two detectives looked at each other.

"Who, sir?" Kerpnacki asked.

"Who Sir?" the Captain mimicked. "You're so fuck'n polite when your asses are on the line." He leaned over and grabbed a sheet of paper. "His name on his passport is Dragon Petrovic."

The detectives shot each other a look.

"Don't know who that is?" The Captain asked. "Of course not. You two have been too busy out on the street. Booking people on murder charges with evidence a kindergartner could demolish."

"That's not fair," O'Brien said.

"Really? What do you have?"

"A neighbor who saw Daniels near the time of death leave Anatoly's apartment. An admission that the murder weapon was hers."

The captain tried to suppress his grin. "Genius, what was the time of death?"

O'Brien shifted his weight. "Well sir, according to Kerpnacki…"

"What?" she yelled. "You told me the medical examiner said early evening."

"Like I said, Captain, my partner gave me the time of death."

The captain held up his hand. "Let me, please. After we had our earlier meeting and I told you about the warehouse on Lake Street, you guys went down to lock-up and grabbed Ms. Daniels. You figured she was involved."

The two detectives nodded.

"You didn't ask Daniels a thing before you threw her into your car?" The captain paused and didn't get a response. "Okay, you took her down to the warehouse, and I'm going out on a limb, she had no fucking idea why or what you were doing." He stopped again and looked at his officers. "When you couldn't get into the place, and she couldn't be of help, my guess, you, O'Brien slapped her. It's all right. Don't say anything." The Captain straightened and looked at the paper he was holding. "Dragon Petrovic, aka Hugo, was found dead in his apartment. A neighbor who com-plained of a strange smell flagged down a beat officer. The medical examiners seemed to think he died more than a day ago. Do you know where Ms. Daniels has been in the last twenty-four hours? I'll tell you…here. She's been locked in a cell. Just to cover all bases, I had Detective Pietowski check with the doorman at Daniels' apartment. This man, Peter something, claims she was home with her husband the day before last.

The captain took a breath. "Anyone want to guess Hugo's cause of death?" He looked from O'Brien to Kerpnacki. "No? I won't keep you in suspense. A bullet wound to the heart."

"I was going to suggest that, sir," Kerpnacki said.

"Sure you were," the captain said. "One more thing. Hugo was found in bed—naked. His hands covering his dick."

Chapter Thirty-Seven

The cell door slid open. "You can go, Ma'am," O.B. said. "You're being released. Captain's orders."

Beth had been sitting on her cot. "I'm what? What did you say?"

"You can go. I have your property bag. All you have to do is sign this slip."

She rubbed her face. It was still sore from the slap she'd received. "I can't believe this. I can't believe this whole fuck'n nightmare." Her lips quivered and her eyes welled-up. She fought for control. After a minute or so she found her voice. "S-o-r-r-y," she said in between sobs. She wiped her face with her hand. "I must l-o-o-k like hell," and after two or three deep breaths forced herself to calm down. "How do I get home?"

O.B. gave her a blank stare.

"My car isn't here. The cops brought me. How do I get home?"

"Well, ma'am, we don't run a delivery service. Dere's the bus out front of the station."

"A bus?"

"Yes, ma'am. Dey run every twenty-thirty minutes."

She must have looked as if she was going to burst into tears again.

"I'll tell you what," O.B. said after a pause, "I'll get you a cab. Just have a seat. It'll take but a minute."

"Thank you. I'd call my husband, but I ..." She searched

her property bag. "My phone. Where the hell is my phone?" She threw her wallet, small purse, and keys out of the plastic folder and onto the floor. "It's not here," she shouted. "What did you do with it?"

O.B hung up and grabbed his clipboard. "Ma'am, be cool, now. Dis is the inventory of your property. Dere is no phone."

"How can…?" She stopped in mid- sentence. "Oh…right. I remember. The female detective didn't let me. Sorry. I'm so sorry."

O.B. gave her a long glance. "It's been quite a time for you. I'll get that cab."

Chapter Thirty-Eight

Joe wished he had his watch. Not only was it expensive, but it… He stared at the empty spot on his wrist. *Damn, where the fuck is Nicole?* He was sure at least twenty minutes had gone by. His fingers didn't move well. The cold had turned them red, or so he thought. He had trouble seeing, as his eyes watered due to the wind and freezing temperature. He'd use Siri instead.

"Hey, Siri, call Nicole."

"There is Nicky's, a restaurant on Madison and Wells. Here is the number."

"Shit. *Siri*, N-i-c-o-l-e. Call Nicole."

"What in Nevada is of interest? Gambling, casinos, prostitution?"

Siri was goddamn crazy or as frozen as he. Between his hand tremors and his body shaking, he labored to hit the right digits to make the call. He heard the line ring several times, then Nicole's voice came on and asked the caller to leave their name and number.

Voicemail? Did she turn off her phone? He huddled in a doorway as much away from the wind as he could. His thinking was becoming fuzzy. He knew he should think of a plan in case…in case. *Not possible. She's probably stuck somewhere. She'll call any minute.* He stared at the phone, willing it to ring. The phone won. *That bitch. She should be here by now.* He peeked out from his meager shelter and looked up and down the street. A car rolled slowly toward him. He moved as quick as he could to the curb. The lights were in his face and he couldn't tell the make or model. Thank God, he was saved. He could almost feel the heater in the car. He'd turn that blower all the way.

"Nicole," he said and waved his arms. "Over here. Thank God. I knew you'd come."

The car drifted and stopped a few feet from him.

"How much?" The voice was male.

"Huh?"

"Man, I'll give you a ten spot. You look like it been a long night." He hung the bill out his window.

Joe took a few steps back toward the doorway. "Sorry, I thought you were…" He heard the car's engine idle. It was the only sound.

The man leaned out the window. "You sure is ugly. No wonder you ain't do'n shit. A man offer you ten dollar and you stand there like I'm talk'n Chinese. Well fuck you. If I sees you on this corner again, dere won't be much of you for the garbage men to pick up in the morning." The car took off, tires screeching.

Joe watched the taillights fade. *Shit, Nicole isn't coming. Think. I have to get the hell out of here.* He gripped his phone. He held it up to his mouth. "Hey Siri, call Beth, home."

A man like him who always had plans, now… Where did he go wrong? He was the best. The best lawyer, the best lover, the… The wind knifed through his thin shirt. He always wanted more…more of everything, especially money. Now, he was on some frigid corner on the west side like a street bum hoping to survive.

***

Beth walked through the deserted lobby of her building. Only Peter the doorman was there.

"Glad to see you Ms. Daniels," he said as a smile crossed his face.

"Thank you, Peter," was all she could say without falling apart.

He opened the door that led to the bank of elevators for apartments.

"Have a good evening."

She nodded and walked past him. Her hand shook as she pushed the Up button. The elevator came almost instantly. She could feel her emotions welling. She dabbed her eyes, not wishing to be seen crying. Another minute or two and she would be home. She covered her face with her hands and waited for the chime that announced her floor. Within the minute or two that it took, the whole awful experience flashed by. *How did this happen? Who was who?*

The elevator stopped and she got off and hurried to her front door. She dug into her purse for the key. With each passing second, her frustration mounted. *What did the cops do with them? Those motherfuckers. They kept them. Damn them.* She gripped her satchel and shook it. She heard nothing that sounded like keys. She stuck her hand through the opening and ravaged the insides. She was about to dump the whole damn thing. That's when she remembered the small pocket within one of the compartments. *Thank God.* She slid the key into the lock and pushed the door.

Home. The sights and smells of it engulfed her. The emotions she'd held in spilled out in a loud sustained cry. It bent her over and she reached for the back of the couch to steady herself. Her Sonny was dead. Her body shook. That sweet man—her lover—gone. But that other name the cops used…Anatoly Dmur…something. How could that be the same person? Was there another game? Another woman? Impossible. Where would he have found the time or the stamina? A slight smile tugged at her lips. *God, he was so good.* She folded her arms across her chest, wishing she were being held. Instead of smelling him, she caught the odors of where she had been, the stench of the lock-up and interrogation.

She tore off her blouse and pants and ran to the bathroom. She didn't wait for the water to turn warm. She let the spray splash all of her. She lathered her loofah and scrubbed her skin until she saw pink blotches. Then she just let the water run and closed her eyes. Sonny's image was in front of her. He smiled and reached out. She saw his hand and stepped toward him.

"Come on," she heard him say. "We will play some more."

"Oh Sonny, where do you get…"

She opened her eyes and saw only the bathroom tiles. She drew a deep breath and finished. Her towels were soft and fluffy. They smelled warm and sweet. She wrapped herself in them and went into her bedroom.

The bed was empty. At first, that wasn't a concern. Then it dawned on her. Where's Joe? It's almost morning. Even he didn't… Then she remembered. *God, is he alive? What hospital?*

Chapter Thirty-Nine

A car was parked in front when Susan cracked open the front door of Hugo's warehouse. She stood in the doorway but was too far away to see if it was occupied. Not taking any chances, she shut the door, leaving enough room for her to see but not enough to be seen. Had that Buick or was it a Chrysler been there? She looked away. Was it an undercover cop? Or the same assholes who had been casing the place? She couldn't stay much longer. It must be after three. She was sure that the fruit and vegetable deliveries as well as the police would be coming early morning. She pulled the door a little wider. That fuck'n car was now down the block. *Huh. Someone was watch'n the front.* She shut and double-locked the door.

She didn't use her flashlight, which made getting to the back slow. Her car was next to Hugo's van parked outside the garage and thirty feet from the rear entrance. Her hands were sweaty. She repeated to herself that she could do this. She unlocked the back and peeked. The vehicles were as she'd left them. No one else was in sight. "Surprise," Dumond taught her, "erased many mistakes." She put her hoodie over her head. With her key in hand, she bent over and ran to her car. Once in, she turned the ignition and peeled down the driveway. She made a right at the intersection and flew by the unsuspecting bastard. She gained a block, then two, then three. There were no lights reflected in her rearview mirror. Whoever that was, didn't follow. Her hands that had tightly gripped the steering wheel, eased, and then a smile played on her lips. She beat whoever those motherfuckers were.

Susan tumbled into her apartment clutching the notebook taken from the warehouse. Even though it was nearly sunrise, she had too much adrenalin to sleep. She went to the kitchen, boiled water for coffee, and flicked on the radio. Her humming of an Edith Piaf song was interrupted by the news. *Que se passe-t-il?* (What the hell?). She glanced at the station and was about to change it, but the water boiled. The kettle continued to chirp even after turning off the flame. She reached for Ethiopian coffee beans and after measuring, placed the beans in her grinder. The smell of the ground coffee evoked recollections of Paris cafes. She sighed and closed her eyes for a second or two, lingering on her memories. There were many lazy weekday mornings when after lovemaking, she and Dumond would dress and walk to a boulangerie off the Champs Élysées. Their breakfast was of the crispest croissant slathered with almond butter and topped off with Parisian coffee. She wrapped her arms around herself and wished to go back in time.

She poured the coffee into the French press on the counter, then added boiling water and applied pressure to the plunger. She watched as it made its way to the bottom. The color of the mixture turned a rich dark brown. Satisfied, she opened a cabinet and took a small Wedgewood cup and saucer. This was a celebration of sorts. She had survived not just the day, but the notebook full of names, and God willing, orders was her ticket. She filled the demitasse and breathed in the aroma. She lifted the cup to her lips filled with anticipation.

"Chicago Police found the body of a man now identified as Dragon Petrovic shot to death in his home on the Northwest side. There was no sign of a struggle. Police are investigating. We'll have the traffic and weather after this."

"Mon Dieu." Her hand trembled. She stared at the radio, at first not believing what she heard. The rattle of the china against the saucer spilled the coffee and brought her back. "Dragon Petrovic..." Her voice trailed off. She put the cup and saucer down, as if they were from a greasy spoon, and grabbed the notebook. She tore through the book searching for that name. It was difficult going. The writing was in a language she didn't understand. "What the hell was this?" As she came to the second to last page, she saw her name and an arrow drawn to Dumond. Staring at her was her order—the number and kind of guns and the cost. On the last page, there were three names: Anatoly Dmursic, Nicole, no last name, and an arrow to Joseph Daniels. That name was underlined in red. She flipped the pages toward the front and saw *Dmursic* listed a few times. There was even a phone number.

Chapter Forty

"Bitch, wake up. You are not at B and B."

Nicole stirred, but did not wake.

"Get up," the man with a short beard said, then shook her.

"Gentle, Boris, honey gets better results." He was clean-shaven and bald.

"She is playing with us, Ivan. We used a mild form of chloroform. She's been out for hours."

They looked at the body whose hands and legs were bound and lay crumpled in the corner of the room.

"Soon, Boris. Nature has a way of awakening even sleeping princesses or bitches. We are all governed by those rules."

"A philosopher." Boris spit on the floor. They had driven to an abandoned house on the southwest side of the city. "After she tells us about Anatoly, I want her before…"

"Of course. Payment for our troubles—one way or another. We will have our reward."

"What do you mean? I don't want to share. She's mine. I have made great sacrifices. That's all there is to it."

Ivan rested his meaty hands on the table. "Let's not argue over the spoils until the time comes. We have a job to do. Are you forgetting we are soldiers in the struggle for our homeland? We must focus on the enemy and traitors."

Boris stroked his beard. He looked over at the woman, then gave a toothy smile. "No, it should be settled now." He took a seat a few inches from his partner.

Ivan let out a breath. "Here, a drink. Vodka. It will calm

your nerves." He reached into his coat pocket, but Boris grabbed his hand.

"I am not stupid."

Ivan stared into Boris's face. "No, you are not." He pulled the trigger and Boris fell over.

Ivan backed away from his fallen associate. Boris was sprawled on the floor. Ivan watched for a few seconds, then got up and kicked him. "Fool, now there is more to do. Shit. As if kidnapping the bitch wasn't enough."

***

The sound of gunfire startled Nicole. She opened her eyes. There was a table, two chairs, and the back of a stocky bald man. Where was she? What was she doing on the floor? Nothing was familiar. She tried to move and was shocked to find her hands bound as well as her feet. Gnawing fear became a torrent and she screamed. The bald man turned. He was short and stocky. There was a hole in his army jacket pocket.

"What have we here? The princess has awoken," he said. "She screams like a baby being born." He put his hand to his lips for her to be quiet.

She gasped and gulped in air. "What…who are you?"

"Where are my manners? I am Ivan. My associate, Boris, would introduce himself, but there was an unfortunate accident."

"Huh?"

"You cannot see. I'll help you up."

He took three steps toward her.

"Please—don't—hurt me. What…do you want?"

"For now, to introduce you." He grabbed under her arm and lifted. "See on the floor."

She followed his gaze.

"Oh my God! Is he dead?" Her heart pounded.

"I'm afraid so."

She tried to pull away, but his grip was too strong. "W-h-a-t d-o...," she couldn't get the words out. She was dizzy and felt like puking. The room was beginning to spin.

He slapped her with his free hand. The force of the slap focused her attention.

"I apologize. I left a red mark on your beautiful face. But you need to gain control of yourself. Hysterical women get me angry, and you don't want me upset."

"What do you want," she was able to say. The words came out in a husky whisper. She felt his stare go through her.

He licked his thick lips, then smiled. He let go of her arm and she sank to the floor.

"What do I want? Such a broad inquiry. Did you ask Anatoly the same?"

"Who?"

Chapter Forty-One

"You come waltz'n in an hour before sunrise? You don't think I'd notice? I've been married too long not to know my man ain't in the bed. What's de excuse this time?"

Billy Dee could sense she was standing over him. He kept his eyes closed. Maybe she would go away. It felt like his head just hit the pillow. "Lord, just a few hours rest. That's all. Amen."

"Don't you be play'n, Billy Dee. I knows you ain't sleep'n. If you was the room be shak'n with your snoring."

"Damn, she good. Hard to fool her after thirty-some years." He lay as still as he could but lifted an eyelid to spy the time.

"Ah hah! I knew you ain't sleep'n. There's a phone call for you. Your police buddy Shep call'n."

He rose instantly. "Janine, why didn't you say that in the first place. All that carry'n on. God have mercy. Where's the phone?"

She stared at him with her hands on her hips. "Where it be all the time—in the kitchen.

"Come on, Janine, the portable."

"You want me to tear my house up look'n so that the king here don't have to move his two feet for the phone?"

He looked at her and knew the argument was lost. "Okay, okay." He got out of bed and shuffled to the kitchen.

"Billy Dee?" Hope I didn't get you in trouble," Shep said before Billy Dee had a chance to say hello.

"Naw, noth'n new. A man is always in trouble," he said with an eye out for his wife.

"You're sink'n in it now."

"Uh huh."

"Did you find out anything last night?" Shep asked, changing the subject.

Billy Dee brushed his face with his hand. "What time is it?"

"About lunchtime, a little after eleven. How late did you stay out?"

"Way more than I should have. Listen, I'll meet you in an hour and we'll grab a bite."

"I'm always up for that. What did you have in mind?"

"Breakfast."

"Break— no problem. How's Tempo on Chestnut."

"Deal." Billy Dee hung up. When he turned, he was staring into his wife's face.

"Breakfast? You don't eat here no more? How come you spend over thirty-five years bitch'n about being a cop and now all you want to do is to be a cop. You one crazy man."

"You right, Janine. Don't understand it myself. But Shep needs my help."

"He do, do he. Last time you did good we were almost all killed."

Billy Dee took her hand. "I know. Every day after, we've been blessed." He looked away. "This case, well, there's a lot of moving parts. That car that blew up yesterday..."

She put her hand up. "Don't tell me. Don't want to know. Just promise not to get hurt. What am I going to do? It's in your blood."

Chapter Forty-Two

Joe put the phone to his ear. *Beth, for once be there.* He listened to the line trying to connect. At least Siri got it right this time. He reflected on his luck, what there was of it. Huddled in a door way, the sky filled with snowflakes, it seemed his fortune went from bad to worse. He was like the ancient Jonah being cast into the sea and swallowed by a whale. But unlike the biblical character, he didn't see repentance as his salvation. *One step at a time,* he told himself.

"Hello?" It was a female voice, but the lack of clarity made it difficult.

"Beth, Beth, it's Joe."

"Joe!" The line exploded with the sound of crying.

"Beth, listen to me." He moved the phone away from his ear. "Calm down, please," he shouted. His command was lost in her hysterics. He would have slapped her if he could. "Damn it, Beth, I'm freezing to death. Shut-up. I'm trying to tell you something."

Her end went quiet but for some sniveling.

"I'm on Lake street not far from Morgan. I need you to pick me up—now."

"Lake and Morgan? What the hell are you doing there?"

He was surprised at how quickly she regained her composure. "I'll explain everything, but you need to get your ass over here. I have no coat. I can't feel my fingers or feet."

"Move my ass? Who are you talking to, one of your playthings? Call them."

"Beth!" He paused and sucked in air. "Please. I mean it. I'm in bad shape—come quick."

"It's four in the morning. I haven't any sleep. I'm not doing well either. The night I've had. I took a sleeping pill to calm myself a half-hour ago. Can't you call a cab?"

He wanted to throw the phone into a wall. "I have no money and no credit cards. If I did, I wouldn't have called."

"Okay, stop yelling. I'm sorry. I'll get you a cab. Give me a minute or two and I'll call you back."

The line went dead. *Shit, here we go again.* He blew on his hands, but it did little good. He had never been this cold in his life. *Come on, come on where is that goddamn cab?*

***

"Where you want to go?" The driver asked in a Middle Eastern accent.

Joe had just gotten into the taxi. His body trembled from the cold. "T-t-t-u-r-n up h-h-e-a-t."

"What about feet?"

"H-e-a-t. H-o-t a-i-r."

"No, fare paid. Where do I take you?"

Joe curled up in the seat. His arms hugged his body to stop from shaking. He looked up and saw the driver watching him in the rearview mirror.

"Are you sick?" The cabbie asked. "If going to puke get out of cab."

"Not… sick. I'm f-r-e-e-z-i-n-g."

"You what? I take you to hospital."

"No. No hospitals" He took a breath. "Put up the heat."

"Sir, heat on. Any hotter and we be cooked."

"Fine… your vest. I've been," Joe swallowed, "in the cold."

The driver turned toward him. "Not my business but don't you know it not summer here.

"Just for a few…minutes."

The driver stared at him seemingly forever. "You want my coat?"

"Please. I'm freezing."

"Okay. Here." He took it off and handed it to Joe.

"Thanks."

"Sure."

Joe wrapped the garment around him. "Okay… better." His shivering slowed. He heard the driver mutter in non-English.

"Where to, boss?" The driver asked not taking his eyes off of him.

Joe eased back in his seat. He thought about the question. "Home," he finally said, "Chestnut and the Drive."

The cab whizzed down the near-empty streets toward the highway. Joe had tucked his hands inside the coat. He could finally feel his fingers. The warmth of the cab allowed him to think beyond survival. Nicole—*that bitch. Left me out in the cold to die.* He couldn't get that thought out of his mind. *What a heartless woman. To think I was going to throw away everything.* The anger warmed him, and he became more himself. "On second thought," he told the driver, "pull up to State and Delaware and wait. It will take a few minutes."

Chapter Forty-Three

Dmursic, Nicole with no last name, and this Joseph Daniels are all tied to Hugo. Customers? Susan went back to the last page of Hugo's notebook. It made sense. Why else would their names be there after hers? She turned to the front of the book. The letters looked like something written in Russian. She went to her desk, flipped on her computer and Googled the symbols. "Hmm, Slavic, meaning guns *Bon*." She looked at her watch. It was almost seven. *Would Dmursic be up?* She took her phone out of her purse and toyed with it. Was that the same man she saw as she left Hugo's that late October evening? Seconds that's all it was. An image she saw from her car who appeared to be someone she had met as Sonny. Mon Dieu, could that have been him? She stared focusing on nothing. *Non, Dumond didn't believe in coincidences.*

She looked back at her cell. It struck her that but for her mobile…this technological leash, she wouldn't be in this situation. If she hadn't forgotten it in Hugo's bedroom—who knows, maybe nothing would have happened to him. He was a good enough fuck. *C'est la vie*. She couldn't undo what happened.

She punched in the number Hugo had written for Dmursic. Her finger hovered over the connect button. "*Non, ce serait stupide*, and the call would be traceable." She put her cell down. Fatigue washed over her. It had been a long day and even longer night. Her last thought before sleep was that nothing linked her to Hugo anymore.

***

The phone's ring woke her. "Allo," her voice smothered in sleep.

"Where are you?" The male voice sounded upset.

"What?" She glanced at the clock next to her bed. "Mon Dieu, it cannot be. 6:00 p.m."

"That's why I'm calling. You should have been here an hour ago. What happened yesterday? You didn't even call."

"Yesterday? I wasn't scheduled."

"Bullshit."

He was difficult to hear over the background noise and his breathing.

"Look, if you're not here in a half hour, you're fired."

"I'll be there." Susan jumped out of bed, showered and dressed in ten minutes. Dumond's plan was for her to get a job until he was ready to move. It wasn't difficult. Her looks and French accent made her perfect to bartend at a posh place in River North.

This wasn't the first time she had received such a call. Jimmy, the manager, allowed her a certain leeway. But, he did sound angrier than in the past. Well, she would have to take good care of him.

Forty minutes later, she arrived. This was the after-work stop for those who wanted to be seen. Men in suits and open collars brushed against women in short skirts and skimpy tops. The money and pick-up lines flowed like smooth scotch at $20 a shot.

"You're late," Jimmy said. They were in the kitchen area away from the staff.

Susan brushed her hair back. "Oui, I am sorry, Jimmy. I'll do better."

He moved closer and grabbed her. "You better." He kissed

her and then slapped her ass. "You owe me, Susan. Don't forget it."

"Of course," she said, "I won't disappoint." She smiled and walked in a manner she was sure he enjoyed. "Jimmy," she turned, "can I use your phone? My battery died."

"You're an hour late and you want to make a call. Jesus."

"Please, I won't be long." She stepped toward him. "Jimmy." She touched his hair and then ran her hand down his shoulder.

"Okay, okay. Who are you calling?"

She put a finger to her mouth. "Ssh…my uncle."

"Uncle? What the fuck?"

She took several steps away from him and reached into the pocket of her jeans. She took out Dmursic's number and dialed.

Chapter Forty-Four

"Ana-toly?" Ivan stared at his prisoner. "Please, do not insult both of our intelligence. I know and you know Anatoly. The question is, why did you kill him?"

Nicole let out a cry. "Kill him? Anatoly dead? I—I. It isn't possible. I talked with…. you must believe me." She looked at him, her eyes wide.

"You look so innocent. Your pretty face has just enough tears, and I see you shaking. Fear or the truth?" He made a *tsk-tsk* sound. His boot traced her leg to her hip, then rested against her stomach." "You had nothing to do with his death?" The pointed tip of his Frye's pressed hard against her.

"No—ah. Please, I had nothing… I can't…breathe."

"Tell me again."

Her mouth was open and she gasped. She tried to wiggle away, but her struggle made it worse. "I…can't…"

"Breathe? Yes, I know. Perhaps sitting would make it easier." He stepped away, then grabbed her under the arms. "Here, my dear, there's a chair next to my former partner. You can commiserate together." He laughed and dragged her to the spot.

He dropped her into the seat. There was blood around the chair. Boris's eyes still had a shocked look as they stared into nothing.

"I'm going to vomit," she said.

"Try not to. Cleaning it up may nearly be the last thing you do."

She felt the nausea rise from her stomach. She gulped several times to keep from throwing up. Sweat dripped from her hairline down her face. With her arms bound, the helplessness added to the descending lightheadedness.

"No, no, you can't faint. Not allowed." He went to the sink and filled a glass.

The water splashed her face.

"Ach, bastard," she screamed.

He pulled her hair. "Manners, please. I'm a civilized man and you, an educated woman. No need for those kinds of foul words." He took out a handkerchief and wiped her face. He stepped to the side and inspected her as if she was an object for sale. "Let's start again." This time his voice was soft. He brushed a strand of hair from her face. "You and Anatoly had a business relationship, yes?"

She nodded.

"Good. This business was guns, correct?"

She hesitated.

He held her chin in his fat hand. "You have a model's chin. What a shame if it was smashed. I hate to destroy beauty, but as my friend Boris found out, sometimes it can't be helped. "One more time, dear, your business relationship…"

"Anatoly and I," her breath came in spurts, "ran a scam on a lawyer and his wife."

"How interesting. Tell me more."

She spoke slowly "We were going to blackmail each of them."

"Explain."

"Really? Anatoly had an affair with the wife and I with the husband. When each found out about the other, we would ask for compensation to keep quiet."

"And did this work?"

"It did, but now… It's all apart."

Ivan took a plastic water bottle from his coat pocket and drank. "I'd offer you some, but…germs. Who's the lawyer?"

"Why is that important?"

He slapped her hard again, across the face. "I ask. You answer. Understood?"

Her mouth was agape. She didn't respond. She hung her head and squeezed her eyes. *Don't cry,* she told herself. Despite that, tears rolled down her face. "I'm sorry," she stammered, "I'm sorry. Please don't harm me. I don't want to be hurt." Her body convulsed. When she looked up, Ivan had a knife in front of her face.

"It's okay. I'm only going to cut the ropes tying your wrists. You'll feel better."

She felt him grab her arms, and in seconds the bounds were loose.

"Use my handkerchief," he said and waited.

She mopped her face slowly. "Thank you," and clutched the cloth in her hand. "You want to know about guns? The lawyer according to Anatoly was into running them. Anatoly wanted to expand our scheme. He had a friend. I can't think of his name, but we went to see him."

"And this friend of Anatoly's was able to get weapons?"

"Yes, I guess. I don't know for sure." She ran her hand over her face and felt the mark left there by Ivan's slap.

"Do you remember where you met this man?"

Her hand rested on her cheek. She stared at Ivan. "No. I mean, I didn't pay attention. Anatoly drove. I-I…"

He moved her hand and studied the bruise. "It will swell," he said, then to himself in Serbian, *if she lives, I should be more careful. Scars and marks reduce value.*

She understood what he said, but not what it meant.

His forefinger touched her face. She sat rigid. "It's okay."

He laughed. "Your skin is soft. I like that. Now back to this person. What is his name?"

"I don't remember."

"You must do better. Unbutton your shirt."

"What?"

"Either you do it, or," he took his knife out, "I'll just use this."

"Okay, okay." She fumbled with each button. "Please," she pleaded, and put her arms across her front.

"His name?"

She stared. Her mouth quivered.

"We will play a game. Anytime you don't answer a piece of your clothing will be removed. Strip interrogation. How enjoyable."

"I don't know. Really. We met once. Oh God."

"Unbutton the shirt."

"Nooo" she screamed."

He grabbed her hair and pulled her head back. "Do it."

Chapter Forty-Five

"Here's the thing," Billy Dee said in between sopping up his over-easy eggs with his toast, "I think a whole lot of shit was go'n on at that Hugo's warehouse. It ain't only sell'n fruit."

"Drugs?" Shep asked, his mouth working over his ham sandwich.

"Not sure. There were notebooks all over the place, most of it in I think Russian."

"Russian? How would you know that? You don't speak or read it."

Billy Dee put the bread down. "No, but I've seen those crazy ass letters on the news." He took a sip of his coffee. "I also found this at the door." He took from his pocket the card from *Allied Storage* that had *2475 D* written on the back.

"What the hell?" Shep asked and put the sandwich down. He took the card and inspected it. "You think this is a locker or storage bin number?"

Billy Dee nodded. He finished his eggs and attacked the sausages along with the fried potatoes. He pointed his fork at his partner. "This Hugo was into something. He was there last night but got away. Couldn't get a good look. He drove too quick."

"How do you know it was Hugo?" Shep asked.

"Who else would it be?"

"Mmm, the person who killed him."

"What?"

"While you were getting shuteye this morning, the police found a body in an apartment. His passport identified the deceased as Dragon Petrovic, but his driver's license had him as Hugo D. Petrovic."

"What was the cause of death?"

"A single shot. Hugo was found naked in bed, his hands on the family jewels."

"One unhappy lover, I guess," Billy Dee said. "Any leads?"

"Not yet. You want a fry? Not good for my waistline."

"You should have ordered a salad. I've got all the potatoes I need. They're all yours. I almost forgot. That Detective O'Brien, the dick you had a run-in with, he also showed up at Hugo's."

"No shit. What for?"

"Don't know, but he and his partner had, I believe, Ms. Daniels with them. From what I saw, she had no idea what their little trip was about."

"Wait a minute," Shep said in between munching his fries, "you saw all of this?"

"Hey, I may be retired, but I still got moves. I hid pretty good. Saw the whole thing. Those fools never got inside the building, just stumbled around for a few minutes, then took off. I waited and as I thought of calling it a night, the warehouse door opened. Whoever that was must have taken a look, went to the back and got the hell out of there."

Shep held another potato between his fingers, ready to dunk it in the ketchup. "That was some night's work."

Billy Dee leaned back. "Not bad for a guy grazing in the pasture. When you're done feeding your face…"

"Watch it. Civilized people call it dining."

"Uh-huh. I think we should take a ride to Allied Storage."

"And do what? We don't have a search warrant."

"Since when did that stop us. We have a badge."

Shep smiled. "I have the badge."

Billy Dee reached into his pocket. "It's ancient but it do fine." He laid his old star on the table.

"I thought you had to turn those in."

"You do." Billy Dee winked.

Chapter Forty-Six

Joe got out of the cab and before he had taken three steps, the cabbie lowered his window.

"Mister…the jacket."

Joe turned. "I'll be right back. I'm going into that building and I'll be gone ten minutes at most."

"Fare does not include vest."

"Come on… ten minutes…"

"No sir, jacket."

"For God's sake, man. I'm not going to keep your damn coat."

"I don't know that. Now please…"

"I could have been back by now. It's still freezing outside." Joe stared at the driver for a second or two, deciding whether he had made his point. When no immediate response came, he headed for the building. He stopped when the cabbie leaned out the car window and wagged his forefinger. "If you not back in ten minutes I bill double."

"Fine, whatever," Joe said, and moved as fast as he could. As he entered the building, the doorman/security person looked up from behind his desk. Newspaper pull-out ads from various stores covered the surface. *Damn, a new guy,* Joe thought. He had been to the building enough times. Security should have known him.

"Can I help you, sir?"

"That's okay, just going to visit a friend. I have a key."

The man's nametag said "Charles." He glanced at his

watch. "At this hour, sir, I believe I should call. Is the friend expecting you?"

Joe could tell that Charles tried not to be judgmental but was aware of what may be going on.

"Yes, in a manner of speaking," Joe said. "I asked to be picked up and I guess there was a delay. I had to call a cab." He turned slightly and pointed. "It's waiting."

Charles peered over his desk. "It appears so." He put the phone down. "Okay, go ahead."

Joe figured that at least three minutes had gone by. Charles buzzed him through the security door. He paced waiting for the elevator, which finally came. It took another minute or so until he was at Nicole's door. *The fuck'n bitch left me out in the cold to freeze.* It played like a symphony in his head. He pressed the doorbell hard and waited. *It's over. Done. And so is her job. Fuck her. He'd take back every damn gift, piece of jewelry, he ever gave her.*

"Come on, Nicole, open the fuck'n door. The game is up." He jiggled the door handle and used his fist, although he had to be careful—neighbors. "Nicole, damn you."

He looked up and down the hallway and then used his key. The apartment was dark. "Nicole, you bitch, wake up. If I find you with another guy—watch out." His lawyerly ability to separate fact from emotion be damned. He flicked on the lights and walked into her bedroom. The bed was unmade, and there was a pile of clothes on the floor. *Where the hell could she be?* He saw a wine glass and bottle in the kitchen. A cabernet sauvignon—the kind he liked. "Huh," he said, trying to make sense. He walked around her place one more time, but she wasn't there. He left disappointed and confused, his walk to the elevator no longer a march but ponderous. *What the hell happened? Did she try to find me? Was she on the west side?* His anger receded, replaced by gnawing guilt. Instead of pressing "1" when the elevator arrived he decided to check the garage. *If her car is still there…*

The garage was bathed in a yellow dim light that illuminated particles of dust. It was like breathing in hazy fog. That stuff couldn't be good for you. He walked down the rows to where she usually parked. His footsteps echoed. Too many damn white cars, although hers, as she'd remind him, was pearl. He couldn't tell the difference. Midway down the row, he mistakenly stopped. It wasn't hers. He looked further and believed he spotted it. He quickened his pace until his foot landed on something hard like a pebble or a rock. It was a fob. As he bent down to pick it up, a jolt of heat shot up his legs. He let out a howl, then steadied himself by putting his weight on his arm. He pressed one of the buttons and heard a beep, then saw Nicole's taillights flash several cars away. "Oh shit." Sweat dripped down his shirt collar. He took a deep breath to block his muscle's resistance as he tried to stand. Something shiny, though, caught his eye underneath the vehicle. "Noo," he said, "couldn't…oh my God." He dropped down and despite his body's defiance, stretched. He came up short a few times. The third, he gave everything he had and grabbed it. He slowly pulled himself up to a sitting position and caught his breath. His back rested against the car's bumper. He squeezed his fist, hoping that what he had in his hand wasn't what he knew it to be. But it was.

Chapter Forty-Seven

Beth looked at the bedside clock. *Holy shit, where's Joe?* She had called a cab for him a while ago, and he still wasn't home. Not that she got much sleep in between. She had shut her eyes, but her mind…played like a reel-to-reel movie. Sonny/Anatoly Dmur…whatever, whirled over her bed, his body and face touching hers. She heard herself moan in anticipation. Then his image disappeared. Sonny morphed into Detective O'Brien and she was in an interrogation room. He told her to undress. Her body stiffened.

"Why?" she asked. What does this…?

"Do it. And shut your mouth." he ordered.

She fingered a button on her blouse. O'Brien became Sonny and nodded to go ahead. She unbuttoned two of them.

O'Brien's bitch of a partner came into the room. Her jaws were going as she chewed a thick wad of gum. "Whatcha doing, O'Brien? Trying to get your rocks off?"

Sonny disappeared.

"What's it to you? She wasn't talk'n. I thought maybe I'd loosen her up."

Sonny came back and winked.

"Great. You dumbass. She talks and you're done…fried like a potato in oil."

Sonny was in the corner of the room, smiling from ear to ear.

"No one's go'n to believe her," O'Brien said as he undid his belt.

Kerpnacki grabbed his shoulder. "Did you forget who her husband is?"

Beth heard herself say, "Yeah. Joe Daniels."

***

She used her arm to search the bed. "Holy shit." She was alone. Her eyes fluttered open. It was 5:00 a.m. The sweat from her nightmare transformed into a sudden chill. She drew the covers around her. It couldn't take an hour to get from Lake and Morgan to here. *Call the cab company? Joe?* She sat up. Where the hell was her phone? It wasn't on the nightstand or in her bed. She looked at the floor and picked it up. She had no memory of dropping it. *Jesus.* The battery marker was in red with 5% left. That meant she had to get up find the charger or use the landline in the kitchen or bathroom. *Damn Joe, damn.*

She walked in her bare feet. There was a knock at the door. *It's gotta be Joe. Thank God, I guess. Wait till I tell him what happened to me. Why is he knocking? The son-of-a-bitch probably lost his key. And he yells at me for doing the same.*

She flipped the lock and concentrated on what she was going to tell him. "About time…" she said as she opened the door to a large Black man with a silly-ass grin.

"You must be Joe's woman." He didn't wait for a response. He stepped inside and closed the door. "Look at you, dressed in almost noth'n, wait'n for your man. Hmm, he has it s-o-o good."

She crossed her arms over her short night shirt. ""Who are you? How did you get up here?" She retreated a few steps toward her bedroom.

"Don't run away. If I wanted some white ass I'd have

grabbed it. No, not interested in pussy. At least, not yet." He smiled and took a long look. "I'd say this, Joe has good taste. The tits ain't bad and the ass is still boss, but you know I've seen him with better." He poured himself into a chair in the living room. "He's been with this pretty young thing. I'd say late twenties early thirties. Now she fine like a fox. The curves on her…my my." He shook his head.

"What do you want?"

There was blood in his eyes. "You given me an order?"

"No," she stammered, "I just…"

"Dat's better. No bitch gives me orders. You straight?"

She nodded and clutched the neck of her night shirt.

"Good, we have an understand'n. Now, Joe should be dragg'n his ass here any minute. I'm reminding him of some business he needs to do…like now."

He lifted himself out of his seat and in one or two strides towered over her. His bony finger drew an imaginary line down her face. "Nice. Soft. Wouldn't want dat to change. No sir. You tell'm dat. Got it."

He opened the front door.

"Wa…t. Who should I say…?"

His laugh echoed down the hall.

Chapter Forty-Eight

"Hugo, his name was Hugo," Nicole said holding the sides of her opened shirt. "Anatoly drove to a warehouse. That's all I know."

Ivan rubbed his chin. "You see, my game bears fruit. I do enjoy it. And you?"

"I...I...?"

"Not very articulate to a simple question. No matter, off with the shirt." He didn't wait for compliance. The garment ripped.

She lowered her head into her chest and whimpered.

"Shut up. Look at me."

She didn't move. *God help me. Someone help.*

He grabbed her hair around his fist and pulled, forcing her to gaze at him. Her heart pounded as she tried to control her tears. "Please... Don't..."

His hand slid down her neck.

"You know what is next. All you have to do is answer. Where was this warehouse?"

She gulped and moved her hands around his wrist. "I... I."

"Final answer?"

She felt his hand's weight on the front of her bra. "Stop...I didn't pay...wait. There were El tracks. I remember... noise of a train." She gasped. Her hands now batting air. "We walked through boxes of fruit, vegetables—all over the place."

"Uh-huh. Good."

His smile didn't reassure.

"I'm doing the best I can," she said. "Your hand…"

"My hand? You haven't completed the answer. Time's up." He gripped the center of the bra with one hand and with the other took a knife sheathed on his belt. The blade went through the silk in one motion. "A shame," he said. He held a part of it in his hand. "Expensive, now it's garbage." He pushed her back into the chair. "Put your arms at your sides."

She squeezed her eyes shut and did as she was told.

"Nice, very nice—firm, round. Good size."

She felt cold even though a few minutes ago she had been sweating. She sensed he was very close, but he hadn't touched her. She squinted.

He put the knife back in its case. "Those,"—he pointed to her tits—"have bought you many things." He waited for a response.

"Ah… I mean," she said after a pause, "I guess."

"Your modesty is a joke. You've already admitted how you used your body. In any case, back to our little game."

"No more. I can't."

He took the bottom of her chin in his hand. "Boris had his own ideas too. He wanted his dessert before he earned his dinner. Too bad for him." He grabbed her face and made her look at the body near her chair. "Now, my little whore, you tell me everything…everything."

She tried to move her legs, but forgot they were bound to the chair. She burst into tears. "I'm sorry," she repeated, "I'm so sorry. Don't kill me." She buried herself in her arms.

She felt his touch on her hair. It was light, meant to comfort. "I'll stop, no more tears," she said, her body still trembling.

He stooped and picked up the handkerchief that had fallen. "Here."

Her hand shook as she wiped her face and blew her nose. "Okay. Anatoly said we could make even more money. He heard a rumor that…" She stopped and swallowed hard. "A rumor that…"

"Go on."

She sat straighter in her seat and stared at a doorknob behind Ivan. "Joe Daniels was into selling guns."

"Who?"

"The man I was going to blackmail. We worked at the same firm—his firm."

"You are very talented."

"Anatoly had set up the meeting with this Hugo. He wanted to use me to meet Joe. I told him I'd think it over. We left and Anatoly drove me home." She shrugged and wrapped her body in her arms. "That's it, all I know."

He clapped. "Well performed. Bravo. And all it took was your tits to be exposed." He pulled her up from the chair.

"What are you doing?"

"You won this round, but the game isn't over. Put your arms behind your back."

"My feet. I can't move."

He grabbed her hands and bound them.

"Why? What did I do? What are you…"

"We'll be going for a ride."

Before she screamed, he smothered her face with a rag and she went limp.

Chapter Forty-Nine

"A llo, dis is Anatoly, I'm out and very about. Give message." Susan gave the phone a quizzical look, and then put it back to her ear.

"There's some business that may be of interest. Call me at the following number and ask for the French one." She pushed end and took a few seconds to think if anything said was a mistake. *It was the best she could do.* She shrugged and then felt a presence on her shoulder.

"Jimmy?"

"Some uncle. That was mysterious."

She faced him. "We speak to each other in code," she said without missing a beat. "What I said, was hello, how are you. Call me back in French." She slapped the phone into his hand.

"Are you serious?" His look half believed her.

She smiled. "Oh, Jimmy, *vous êtes très cher.*" She gave him a small kiss on the cheek and went to work.

***

It was past the rush and the scene settled down. A group of men sat at one end of the bar, with two to three women interspersed between several couples. Then there were those by themselves.

"Hey, sweet thing," a man called out, "I'm thirsty." He

held up an empty glass. Susan had been speaking to another customer and walked over.

"I think you've had enough," she said.

The man, who seemed to be in his mid-forties with a short haircut, disagreed. "*Au contraire. Je bois comme un poisson.*"

"That is a stupid saying," she said in English. "Fish don't drink anything. They swim… in water."

"Aren't you impressed by my French ?"

She studied him for a minute. "It is no more than high school… taught badly. Your accent…" She looked at the ceiling and then at him. "Your accent is …um… French Canadian. But you are not from Quebec or Montreal. It is more small-townish."

"*Très bien.*" He clapped. "I am from a town called Hudson near Montreal."

"Hudson ? That is New York, no ?"

"Maybe, but I am Canadian. Honest."

Susan smiled despite being unsure. *Is this a trap or a man who wants company ?* "You win," she said, "what are you drinking ?"

"You can guess my accent, but not my drink ?"

She glanced at his glass. "Monsieur, you were drinking scotch and it was expensive. I only asked to make sure you didn't want something else." She straightened.

He focused on her chest for a brief second. "Right again," he said, "sixteen-year-old Belvenie. No cubes…neat. You are good." He gave her a long look. "Incredibly good," he said as if he were a judge at a beauty contest.

She took a few steps to retrieve the bottle. His eyes never left her. She gave him a good pour. *Jimmy won't be happy with my excess. C'est la vie. This could get interesting.*

She brought the glass to him and leaned. "I know."

He lifted the glass. "I wish to make a toast to you, but I don't know your name."

Smooth, she thought. Well, no harm in first names. "Merci. It's Susan."

He held his drink slightly off the surface of the bar. *"Vous ferez un excellent espion."*

She froze. "What ? Spy ?"

"To the Irish for inventing Scotch," he said after tasting a fingerful. His blue eyes never blinked but held her. "You are every bit what Dumond described. I bring a message."

Chapter Fifty

"This the place?" Shep asked, as he turned into a lot across the street from a large single-story building that stretched a block.

"Well, it ain't Wrigley Field. I told you the address," Billy Dee said.

"That's just it. Where the hell's the number? There's no sign, no noth'n."

"I'm sure it's somewhere. Just can't see it from here."

Shep stared him down.

"If Google maps says dis the place, then it is."

They got out of the car and waited to cross the street.

"Where the hell is the front door?" Shep asked.

"Man, you want everything handed to you. We'll get to the other side and check it out. There's got to be a door… somewhere."

They walked around the building. No door.

"This can't be right." Shep said, scratching his head. "Damnedest thing. How the hell do you store shit if you can't get in."

Billy Dee turned the corner. "Yo, found something."

Shep walked to where his partner stood. He looked at the solid wall and then at Billy Dee "What the fuck is this? What did you find?"

"The door." Billy Dee's grin went across his face.

Shep looked from Billy Dee to the bricks in front of him.

"Is this like a *Harry Potter* movie? There's a third dimension or somethin'?"

"Dang. Look down—over here." Billy Dee pointed. The door was below 3 stairs.

"Holy shit. A door. What are you waiting for?"

"Hmm… a key. And since you and I ain't got one, the sign say we need to go to 4000 W. Waveland."

"Shit."

***

"Can I help you?" the middle-aged woman said.

Shep flashed his badge.

The woman sat up straighter. "Yes?"

"I'm Detective Sheppard from Bomb and Arson and …" he pointed in his partner's direction.

"Billy Dee Jackson, ma'am." He took out his star. "I hope'n you could help us."

The woman looked at the star, then at Billy Dee. "There's nothing I can do unless you have a subpoena. My hands are tied."

Billy Dee rubbed his chin. He saw his partner shift his weight. Shep was about to explode. "Now, Ms…?"

"It's Mrs… Stockton. I've been married for twenty years."

"Well me and my Mrs. are going on thirty."

The woman looked away. "I don't think I'll make that number."

"Really?"

" What do you want?"

"My partner and I have been investigating the bombing of that downtown parking lot the other day, and we came across this card." He placed it in front of her. "See the number on the back 2475 D? Is that a storage locker?"

She ran her finger along the edges.

"Ma'am, I mean Mrs. Stockton, it's an innocent question. The answer isn't a…"

She held up her hand. "I know how this goes, Detective. One question begets another until innocence is left standing alone at the station. So, don't patronize me. I've been doing this a long time."

"Mrs. Stock…"

She hit several keys on her computer and looked at the screen. "That number is for a locker at our facility on Clark Street. That's all you get."

"Thank you," Billy Dee said, and took the card from her. "But while you've got the computer on…"

She hit another key. "All gone, Detective."

Shep was out the door. Billy Dee stopped at the threshold. "Mrs. Stockton, are there cameras at that facility?

She looked up from her desk. She paused, then spoke. "All the way around the building and inside. Everything is videoed and kept for thirty days. Anything else?"

"No ma'am. Good to know. You wouldn't happen…"

"Subpoena, Detective. Have a good day."

Chapter Fifty-One

Questions raced through Joe's mind. *What happened? Who would want to snatch Nicole? Why?* He slowly got up, then staggered. He reached out to regain his balance. *My God, what has happened?* Beads of sweat rolled down his face. *Not a good time to pass out.* He held onto the trunk of the car until he felt more stable. He used the back of his hand to wipe his face. *Gotta start walking. Gotta get out of this place. One foot after another…that's it.* He got to the garage door and opened it. The early morning sun blinded him, but the air felt good. He took a deep breath. *Nicole, shit, what do I really know about her? Kidnapped? Or arranged disappearance?* He gazed down the street, not looking for anything in particular but looking. Something—a telltale sign. *Why her? Was it random—wrong place at the wrong time?* He closed his eyes and saw her. *That body. That goddamn body. She certainly knew what men…I liked.* The sound of a truck's gear shift made him look. *She was smart. Picked up on things quickly. I should walk away. Go home and bang Beth and call it a day. Life was complicated before Nicole. Don't need any more problems.* He slipped her bracelet into his coat pocket, then shaded his eyes. *Shit, my cab, where the hell was it?*

"Over here. You longer than ten minutes. I move," the driver shouted.

Joe turned and saw the cabbie waving his arms and went toward him.

"What you do? The driver asked.

"Huh?"

"The back—filthy."

Joe looked over his shoulder. "What are you talking about?"

The driver placed his hands on Joe's shoulders and pulled the coat off him.

"Hey, stop. I'll give you your goddamn jacket," Joe said, "I don't want it."

"You pay cleaning," the driver brushed dirt off the vest and pointed to oil stains. "See…ruined. This expensive. Real down."

"Okay, whatever… add it to the bill…just take me home." Joe went toward the cab.

"Hey, give me cash." The cabbie caught up to him.

Joe stopped. "If I had money we wouldn't be here. Put it on the charge."

The driver held the garment as if it was diseased. He wagged his finger. "No. Cash or you walk."

"Look buddy, I'm sorry for the vest. I don't have money on me. Take me home and I'll give you what you want."

The cabbie roughly crumpled the garment into a ball, placed it under his arm ,and hurried to his taxi. He rolled down the window as Joe neared. "You ruined…"

He took off, leaving Joe in the middle of the street.

Joe watched. The coldness of the morning air that moments ago refreshed now pierced through his thin shirt. "Shit." *At least the apartment wasn't too far—six blocks or so.* Compared to what he had been through, the distance was a snap. He put his hands in his pants pockets and began to walk. His body, though, didn't agree. His legs cramped and he labored to breathe. Sweat and the wind attacked. His home now might as well have been miles away.

***

"About time. Where the hell were you? I called a million times," Beth said as Joe entered the apartment.

He didn't answer.

"You look like shit. I didn't know what happened to you."

He struggled to find a chair and fell in.

"I spent the night in jail. Say something, you prick."

He looked up. "What?"

"I...I... never mind. A black man came here earlier looking for you."

"What are you blabbering? What Black man?" He bent over to catch his breath.

"I don't know who. He said he knows you. Who is he? He scared the hell out of me.

Joe covered his ears. "Shut up will you and get me some water. Did you get a name? What did he look like?"

"He was big and had a beard, and no he wouldn't say who he was."

"Probably a client, that's all."

She didn't move. "A client?" She didn't let up. "He said you've been out with a woman. Who is she? Who's the whore you've been with all evening. Blonde? Young? Damn you."

This was too much. If he had a gun... "Listen," he said in between breaths, "I don't know... anything... about a... woman... I'm hurt...bomb..."

She blinked and her mouth twisted. It was as if she'd been slapped. "Oh Joe, I'm so sorry. I saw. I mean I heard. I've been so worried. You have to lay down. Come on, I'll help you to bed." She touched his arm. "You're so cold." She helped him out of the chair and led him to the bedroom. "Get under the covers. It's okay to keep your clothes on. You'll be warm and you need rest."

She closed the door and the room was dark. The warmth of the bed felt so good. He adjusted the pillows and closed his eyes. He began to drift. His hand rested on his pants pocket. A thought squirreled through his consciousness. He opened his eyes, then patted his pocket. He sat up. The bracelet. With a start, he remembered. He left it in the cabbie's vest.

Chapter Fifty-Two

Something bumped Nicole and it felt cold, then whatever it was went away, until it happened again. She didn't have the energy to investigate. The ebb and flow of stop-and-go movement enticed a return to sleep. But the urge was interrupted by an awakened consciousness. She concentrated on sounds and identified the gear shifts of an engine. Her mouth was exceptionally dry. She tried to shift her position, but she was on her side with her arms bound behind her and her legs tied. There was something across her face and in her mouth.

Her eyes fluttered opened. She gasped. In the darkness, she saw a form inches from her head. She looked closer and identified a face… white with blank but open eyes. *Boris, my God.* The gag muffled her screams. *No, no.* She squeezed her eyes to block out the image and her tears. She was in the grip of a monster. *What does he want? What will he do to me?* She arched her body as best she could to move away. The cold from the metal floor beneath added to her misery and discomfort. She twisted her hands and feet. The bonds around her hands dug into her skin. Instead of loosening, they became tighter; her fingers tingled and grew numb. In her struggle, she wasn't aware there was no more engine noise. Only when she heard a door close did she realize the change. Seconds later, she heard a snap and light flooded the inside of the van.

"I hope you enjoyed your trip," Ivan said.

Her body shook, as she felt her ankles grabbed and her body pulled toward him. He lifted her over his shoulders like a box of water bottles from Costco and carried her. All she could see was the ground.

As soon as they passed a threshold, she heard a motorized door close. He took a few more steps and put her down. *Carpet.* Before she could react, he flipped her on her back, and straddled her. He took the gag from her mouth and placed a finger to his lips as a sign to be quiet. This was terror. She couldn't scream even if she wanted. Her throat and mouth were parched. *What does he want?* She watched him hover over her. Her shirt no longer covered her.

"You stink," he said. "You smell like an unwashed horse. So, here's what we're going to do. There's a very nice shower here. The water is warm and the towels are soft. All you have to do is tell me about this lawyer you were going to blackmail."

Give up Joe, that's all I need to do. She felt her eyes mist. She could barely get the words out. "Joe? You…want…to… know?"

"Exactly." He pulled her into a sitting position. "Water?"

She nodded her head.

He took a bottle from his coat pocket. "Slowly, or you'll choke." After two sips, he capped it. "There's more, but first… and yes, we are still playing our little strip interrogation game." He looked at his watch.

She went into a coughing fit.

"That's all you've done for the last ten seconds. You may be losing this round." He took out his knife.

"I'm…tr..y..ing." Her chest heaved both from fright and lack of air.

"It's up to you."

She saw his knife hand reach for the top of her pants.

"Joe Daniels," the name tumbled out. "Big law firm, knows everyone. He's married."

"I already know that. Go on."

"Please, I will, but the knife…"

"This,"—he held it up to her eye level—"makes you nervous?"

She nodded.

"Good. You haven't said anything for the last five seconds. Talk."

"I don't know. What…what… do…"

"Wrong, wrong answer. You are making it so much harder on yourself." He pulled her up to a standing position and shoved her so that her back was against a wall. The point of his knife touched her skin above the belt line of her pants.

Her scream welled up in her throat. "No…please…no…"

His other hand went around her throat.

Her plea turned into a whimper and she wet herself.

With the knife hand, he ripped the front of her jeans. "See how careful I was? No skin, just the cloth. The back of the jeans will be next. Talk." He removed his hand from her throat.

She was desperate. She had to survive. "Okay. I found…I mean… I knew…Joe was…selling guns."

"Who was he selling them to?"

"I…I …don't…" She fixated on his knife hand. She wanted to sink down onto the floor. Her legs were wobbly and would give out any minute. But terror immobilized her. "If I tell you, will you leave me alone?"

He rubbed his chin, then laughed "That is a good one. I could lie, but there is no need. Let's just say you will suffer less, beginning with that shower."

"Shower?"

"I am a man of my word. It is very nice. I've used it myself. Now Joe sold guns to …?"

"Clients. I don't know exactly, who. There was an Andre or Bug, I think. They could be the same persons or separate.

I… I never saw them or met them. Please, let me go. I've told you everything."

He patted her face, then sniffed. "You smell of piss. Here's how this will work." He took her by the arm and half dragged, half walked her down four stairs. She was in a large room. There was a bed, a chair, two dressers, but no windows. He left her to stand near the bed. He opened a drawer and took out something metal.

"Now, this will go around your neck. It will be attached to this leather strap. If I think you are up to something, I will pull. The choker will contract and you will find breathing difficult." He placed the necklace on her. "Comfy? Not too tight, yes?"

"No." She tried to twist her neck muscles.

"Don't do that. The metal will constrict."

She stopped.

He attached the leash and gripped the end in his hand. "Behave or I will choke you to death." He undid the rope around her legs and then her arms.

She rubbed her hands against her side as circulation returned. There were welts on her wrists and hands where the rope had been.

"Give me your arm." He inspected the bruises. "Your ankles probably have the same. You're young and will heal. Through that door is the shower." He pointed, then pulled on the strap to make it taut. "Where does this Joe Daniels live?"

She saw herself as many things, some worse than others, but never this. *Am I sending Joe to his death?* She hesitated. The metal began to dig into her skin. *Survive,* she told herself.

"Do you understand the question?"

She stared at him. *What can I do?* "P..l..e…e..s..e, it's… hurting… me."

"Precisely. You're so close to comfort. Don't throw your chance away."

She began to wheeze. She held up her hand. "Okay, I'll…
tell…"

He let up on the pressure. "An excellent decision."

"209 E. Chestnut, unit 3805."

"See, not so hard." He loosened the choker. "Enjoy."

Chapter Fifty-Three

I *should get an Academy Award*, Beth thought as she filled a glass with a white viognier. *That black shit probably thought he scared the hell out of me, and Joe…?* Beth sat in her living room and stared out the window at Lake Shore Drive and the lake below. It was late morning and Joe was still asleep. She had double-locked the door.

It felt good to sit and taste good wine. To keep her mind off the present, she got her scrapbook from the guest room. There were playbills, pictures, and reviews from her acting days at Northwestern. She had considered the stage as a career. Then she'd met Joe. Was it the largeness of his wallet or the bulge in his pants? In either case, theatre became less important. They jet-setted the world…the Ritz in London, the Four Seasons in Paris, and the Plaza in New York. At Bergdorf, they ran into celebrities like Dustin Hoffman. Joe made the introductions. Hoffman was polite, Joe called him a "jag off" when everyone moved on. Now she doubted Joe really knew him. Their wedding, in contrast to their courtship glitz, was modest…very. City Hall did the honors with a reception at Riccardo's for ten.

She flipped a page and saw a picture of herself as one of Tevye's daughters in the school's production of *Fiddler on the Roof.* She had a dark wig and wore a skirt to her ankles. *A shtetel girl.* The reviews praised her acting and singing. Two Hollywood, or were they New York, producers gave her their cards.

She thought she heard a sound from the bedroom and looked up. She listened but there was nothing else. She glanced at the book on her lap and took another sip of wine. She should have paid more attention to the words of her song in *Fiddler* ...a girl could get burned...

Marriage ... more like war and peace. After the dawn of a glimmering future came change. At first, minor, like a fly buzzing that's brushed away. The dissatisfaction subtle and barely noticeable. Joe's a little late for dinner. There are fewer calls during the day. Then the bedroom becomes a place for only sleep. She understood either she made an accommodation or the door. She chose the former. He still provided. Why give that up? She took lovers... long before Sonny. The thrill of being wanted and thought of as sexy and attractive was some consolation for being Mrs. Daniels. But even that grew tiresome and worse—unfulfilling. She saw Joe, who once was her knight, turned into someone crass. His shiny armor rusted, covered in filth, and mismatched despite $1,000 suits. He did whatever it took. That applied to his law practice, to the women she was sure he bedded, and to her. Was it because he could? Or was it payback to her?

Her attention drifted to a boat on the horizon. She'd seen enough Novembers in the city to know it was past the season to be out on the lake. It must be one of the last sailing ships making it to winter's harbor. At least whoever that was recognized the peril.

She got up and peeked into where Joe slept. He was still out. She closed the door and went for her coat. He wouldn't miss her if he got up before she was back. She had things to do. Hate is a funny thing. It is destructive, but purposeful. Like love, it's all consuming and clouds out all else. *Joe Daniels, Mr. Bigshot, Mr. I got the City by the balls, well....* She caught sight through the window of the boat nearing shore, then she left.

Chapter Fifty-Four

"Dumond? Why should I know that name? I don't even know yours." Susan wanted to grab this pseudo French-Canadian man's drink and chug it. Instead, she cocked her head.

He gave a half smile. "*Excusez-moi, je m'apelle Jacques Bermais Ernest Jermont.*"

"Jacques and-all-that Jermont? What's it in English?"

"Jack Monte." He flashed a credit card.

She studied the plastic. "Bank of Nova Scotia? This means nothing."

"All true, except you do know Dumond and so do I. When do you finish?"

She looked around for Jimmy, her manager. Not seeing him she said, "We close around two. Give me your number and I'll call."

"Is that a promise?"

She put a hand on her hip. "Listen, Jack or Jacques, you come here out of nowhere and mention a name that I may or may not know. I'll call after I've checked you out."

"Don't take your sweet time. Dumond asked me to find you."

"We'll see."

He got off the stool, finished the drink, then put two twenties down. "That should take care of it." His gaze lingered at her chest an instant too long, then looked up. "At least I didn't ask you to bed."

"The night isn't over."

***

Susan worked the shift with an eye on the clock. Business slowed long before closing. *Should I send Dumond a message? Why would he answer if he hasn't until now? But who else is there?* She took out her phone and stared at it. The use of the cell would leave an electronic trail, but what if Jermont /Monte was not a friend. She weighed the pros and cons and decided to do it. Despite her frequent checks, there was no reply. A little after midnight, with only three people drinking, she decided to give her duties a rest and find Jimmy. She went to the kitchen area. "Have you seen Jimmy?" she asked the cook.

"Ain't seen him since early on. Cheryl be by the dining area. You know how he be. Can't keep that boy away."

"True, I'm sure Cheryl can take care of herself."

"Oh, she can, but do she want to," he laughed.

Susan peered out the kitchen door toward the tables. There were four people seated at one. The rest of the place was empty. Great. Cheryl could finish for her. She took the stairs to the basement and the office. The door was closed, but she heard noise. *Jimmy must be at it again. What a horny bastard.* She felt a tinge of jealousy. Cheryl wasn't bad looking but not like her. She could feel her cheeks flush. *What foolishness. At least Jimmy wouldn't be wanting any from me after he finished with her.* The noise stopped when she was a few feet from the door. *As they say in the trade, that must have been a "quickie," better go.* She jumped when she felt a tap on her shoulder.

"Have you seen the boss man?" Cheryl asked. "I have a headache and want to leave early."

"*Sacré bleu*, I thought you… what? Aren't you with Jimmy?"

"Why would I be looking for him, then? I thought he was with you."

"Me?"

"Oh, please." She gave a dismissive look.

Susan let the implication pass. "I heard noise from the office. He must be there."

Cheryl brushed by Susan and twisted the door handle. "Jimmy," she called. She opened the unlocked door. "It's dark. You sure you heard someone?"

Susan nodded. "I thought it was the both of you. That's why you scared the hell out of me." She reached in and felt the wall for the switch. The light revealed several file drawers opened with their contents strewn on the floor. A pair of shoes stuck out between a cabinet and a desk. "Holy shit, what happened?"

Susan saw Jimmy sprawled on the ground and rushed over. "Jimmy?" There was a gash on the back of his head. She bent down and felt for his pulse. He groaned. "Cheryl, get some ice." She looked up and saw her friend staring at the rear exit. "What are you doing?" She glanced from her to Jimmy, then got off her knees. "*La merde quelqu'un passe la porte* (Holy shit, someone is running out the door)."

Chapter Fifty-Five

Nicole stood under the shower, not moving. She didn't know or care how much time passed. The warmth and pressure of the multiple sprays felt good against her skin. It was almost enjoyable, but for the fear of what comes next. When she mustered the courage to open her eyes, she saw an array of soaps and shampoos with French names lined on a tray. *Where the hell am I?* She was careful with her movements, as the choker was still around her neck. *He was probably watching from somewhere.* She immediately covered herself with her hands, then thought that a useless act. The soaps smelled flowery and she used liberal amounts. Her skin stung where the ropes had chafed. *At least the sores are cleaned and hopefully not infected.* A tug pulled her away from one of the sprays. She watched the suds flow off her and down the drain. Then came another. She had no choice but to follow. The water kept running as she stepped out. Her teeth chattered from the sudden cold of the room. As she went to grab the towels that had been laid out, heater lights turned on. The shower area brightened. The towels were soft, just as Ivan had said. She wrapped herself in one and her hair in another. She looked around for her clothes. Another pull on her neck forced her back into the room where she had been. She remembered there was a bed. It took a minute to adjust to the dimness. When she looked, the bed was empty. Her sense of relief vanished when she heard voices. She glanced over and saw Ivan sitting on one chair and another man on the other.

"Did you enjoy your shower?" Ivan asked.

She didn't respond, only stared.

"It's not polite not to answer. I'll ask again."

She nodded.

"Better," he said and stepped toward her. He tucked her chin into his large palm. "Soft, very nice. Unwrap your hair."

She undid the towel. Her hair was still wet and, she imagined, stringy. Ivan pushed her toward the seated person. "She smells sweet and fresh." He inhaled and let out his breath. "Can you tell, Georgie?"

The other man smiled and slapped his leg. "You are a devil, Ivan. You unwrap your merchandise like the best chocolates, but the rest can wait."

The men switched to Serbian. "Has she given you the information you wanted?" Georgie asked.

"Yes, I think she has told me all she knows." He patted the back of her head. "I don't know who killed our Anatoly but we now may have a way to get guns."

"Good news. Remember, we are soldiers fighting to liberate our land."

"I know that well," Ivan said. "That's why I called you. She can be used for morale and to raise cash for our cause. Our men need rewards when we are short of funds."

"You have a point. She could be used for a while, then sold. Either way, we accomplish our goals." Georgie spit on his hands and rubbed them together. "Well, Ivan, time to unwrap the candy."

"Here is the leash, my friend, you may have the pleasure."

Georgie took the leather strap. "Take the collar off. Such a lovely piece should be unencumbered the first time she is seen."

"You sure?"

"There are two of us. Where can she go? Besides, she is half my size."

Ivan hesitated, then shrugged. "Okay, try her out, then we will work the details." He took off the metal necklace and tossed it on the floor.

He slid his arm around her waist. "Do your best," he whispered in English, "it will go much better. I'll be in the next room."

Georgie stood and let his great coat fall to the floor. He unbuttoned his shirt, and the folds of his fat fell over his belt. She closed her eyes and her body trembled as she felt his hand on her face. Tears dripped. She smelled garlic and cabbage on his breath as his finger traced her lips and then sopped up her cries. "High cheek bones and skin as creamy as butter. I like that."

She opened her eyes when he leaned over her shoulder. Then felt him lick her ear.

"Listen, my bitch," he said softly in English with an underlying threat, "you will fuck me. Understand. You will fuck and do it with energy." He grabbed her head with one hand and with the other pointed to the bed. "How long we let you live depends on it."

She was in a movie that was on fast forward. The star for the moment, who screamed for a new script. The floor was sinking beneath. Her mouth quivered and she gasped for breath. She pleaded to herself, "Please, please, let me survive."

"Okay, my bitch, it is time to unwrap this beautiful package." He undid the towel and let it drop. He stood in front of her and inspected. Then he squeezed her tits. "Ivan was right. Turn around."

She did as she was told. The feel of his hand down her lower back and ass sent chills. Her knees almost buckled. She gritted her teeth and covered her front with her hand. "Yes," he said in Serbian, "she will be worth a good price."

"Get on the bed," he ordered.

She took a step and was about to lie down.

"No, no, on all fours with your ass up, and do not look at me."

She heard the clump of his footstep. Then the unbuckling of a belt, and the zipper of his pants. She closed her eyes tightly. *Oh God let me live, let me live.* She felt him rubbing against her. He used his fingers in a clumsy attempt to stimulate her. His breath rapid. He hadn't entered, but then she felt his hand on the small of her back. She couldn't help herself and stole a glance. Even in the dim light, she saw his face flushed and sweating. She looked away.

He poked her but missed. He swore in Serbian and grabbed her. He tried again. The thrust sent her forward and she had to clutch the bedspread not to fall off. Again, she felt him strike her pubic bone. She slid forward from his force and was grabbed back. He swore and slapped her ass. "I will fuck you, bitch," the words partially in English. He let out a gasp as he pulled her to him. The sound made her look. He had a hand around his dick, the other by his chest. His eyes wide but unfocused, he collapsed next to her.

Her heart raced as this giant lay motionless with his pants at his knees. She looked wildly around the room, then at the door. She sat up and saw his gun hanging from his belt. She grabbed it.

Shit, better do something, Ivan is probably listening? She lay back and panted, her moans loud enough to be convincing. After a minute or so, she stopped. She jumped off the bed and crouched by the side. Georgie was above and in front of her. She placed her hands at the edge behind his torso in the shooting position she had seen on TV and pointed the gun. *To my liberation. Open that door, you bastard.*

Chapter Fifty-Six

"That was productive," Shep said. "We drove all over the damn city to get blown out by 'I-love-my-job' Mabel."

"Stockton," Billy Dee said, "her name was Mrs. Stockton."

Shep glared at him as they walked back to their car. "What the hell… Stockton? We still don't know diddly about who and what is stored at the fuck'n storage place."

"Think of it as a puzzle. We get the pieces and there will come a time when it all fits."

"Since when did you become a philosopher?"

"Retirement. There's more time to think."

"Yeah?"

Billy Dee tapped his pockets. "I need a smoke."

"You ain't goin' to smoke one of your macanudos in the car, philosopher or not."

"Man, you're gett'n to be a pain like my old lady. Seriously your cancer sticks are okay, but a stogie isn't?"

They stared at each other.

"Okay, no cigar, but tomorrow I'm driving."

"We'll see. Where to now, Inspector Clouseau?" Shep asked.

"I'll ignore your dig. Let's go back to Daniels' apartment. And for your information, the *Pink Panther* movies made my sides hurt from laugh'n. Even the wife thought they were funny."

"Great, and why are we going there?"

"Because it is a new day. Beth Daniels may have been

released or maybe the husband returned. We'll never know if we don't."

They got into the car and Shep turned the ignition. "I'm only doing this because there's some great eating joints around their place. That's for the record."

"Noted. Let's go."

Chapter Fifty-Seven

Ivan heard muffled sounds from the next room. He was sure Georgie was enjoying the girl. When Georgie finished, he wouldn't care about the money he'd spend to keep her. Turning a dollar was Ivan's forte, and he'd be paid well. He heard the springs of the bed creak and smiled. Georgie was an oaf but a powerful one. He could choke you to death with one hand while eating a sandwich with the other. A bad man not to have on one's side.

That brought him to how to explain Boris. Georgie would ask. He had forgotten how Boris and Georgie were related, but knew they were. When that time came, Ivan had a story in mind. He would make Boris a hero who died for the cause. The girl who Georgie just fucked had tried to escape and, in the melee, Boris was killed. Ivan arrived too late to save him but recaptured the girl. When they got to this safe house, he called Georgie.

He chuckled as he envisioned the scene. Georgie's face growing red, his eyes narrow into slits and his huge hands balled into fists. "Killing her is too good," he'd say. In Ivan's mind, Georgie unclenched his hand. "Did you not enjoy her? Think about our men." It wouldn't take much to persuade him. The final touch, "Boris would want you to enjoy her." Yes, all neatly done.

The sound of the girl's moans came through the wall and interrupted his thoughts. *The girl is even getting off on this. God does work miracles. Such a whore.* He glanced at his notes from the girl's interrogation. Time to get back to work. He opened his disposable cell. While punching in a number, he thought maybe his finder's fee should be a romp with the girl. A fitting end to the whole business. His growing desire dissipated as he heard a groggy voice through the phone.

"Hello?"

"You don't know me," Ivan said, "but I have a proposition for you."

"Who the hell is this?"

"That is no way to talk to a potential customer, Mr. Daniels."

"How do you know my name? Who is this?"

"The name makes no difference, but your girlfriend has told me about your little business."

"Girlfriend? Nicole? Where is she? I don't understand."

"You will." He gave a little laugh. "Nicole is very good company. You have excellent taste."

"What have you done? I want to speak with her."

"At the moment, she is indisposed. Don't worry, she is fine. She is doing what she does best. But we are going, how you say, off the track. Guns, Mr. Daniels, that is the subject."

"I don't know what you are talking about."

"I understand your reservation, particularly over the phone, but you will." Ivan heard a thump like someone falling from the other room. "We'll be in touch very soon." He hit the End button and got up from the chair.

"Georgie?" He put his hand on the doorknob. "Georgie, she is gold, yes?" He said in Serbian. Silence. His hand went to his hip and clutched the knife handle. "Did she tire you out? Say something?"

He flung the door open. It took a second or two to adjust to the dimness. Within that timeframe, he recognized Georgie on the bed, then saw a flash and as he fell, heard a loud bang.

"You…you shot me." His hand covered his stomach. "I don't understand."

Nicole stood up from her crouched position. She stepped toward him, her arms outstretched but unsteady. "I was aiming for your head. You bastard." She stood several inches from his feet.

He wheezed as he looked at her standing naked. "Be a good whore and suck me off." His laugh turned into a cough. "How far do you think you'll get, my little prostitute? Others will come searching for you. You won't be as lucky with them as you were with me. You will have a slow death. I assure you."

"Shut up. Where is this godforsaken place?"

He pulled himself up into a semi-sitting position. "Can't help you." He glanced at his watch.

"Why did you do that?" she asked.

He grimaced and stared at her. Even as the pain grew, his muddled head desired her. He raised his bloody hand and motioned for her to come closer. "I'll tell you."

Chapter Fifty-Eight

S usan ran toward the rear door of Jim's office. She focused on the shadow that escaped to the outside.

"Watch out," Cheryl screamed.

Her foot hit something and she went sprawling to the floor and landed near the end of the aisle twenty feet from the back exit.

"Are you okay?" Cheryl asked.

She didn't respond. The wind was knocked out of her. After a few seconds, she gasped, "I'm not sure." Pain shot up her leg. "*Merde, merde.*" She forced herself into a sitting position. "*Fils de pute,* son of a bitch."

Jim's moans redirected her attention. She saw Cheryl grab him under his arms and help him sit.

"What happened?" Cheryl asked.

He limply waved his hand. "Not now. I feel like shit."

"I'll get that ice for both of you."

"Good idea." Susan grasped a storage shelf to pull herself up. She hobbled toward the back exit and looked out. There was nothing to see. Whoever whacked Jim was long gone. She slammed the metal door and bolted it locked.

"Here's a couple of compresses," Cheryl said on her return. Susan could see her friend drop one of the bags and then inspect the gash to the back of Jack's head. "Wow that's nasty." Cheryl pressed the compress to his wound.

He grimaced and grabbed the ice from her. "That hurts like hell."

"Sorry. I think we should go to the hospital. You may need stitches."

Susan gimped over to where the other two were. "What about me?"

"Someone's got to stay and close," he said and looked directly at her.

She threw her hands in the air. "Close? I can barely stand, much less walk.

"Then you couldn't drive. The keys are on my belt. Take the night's receipts and put them in the safe."

"And where is that?"

He pointed to an area behind his desk. "It's open. I only close it at night."

"*Fils de pute*," she said under her breath.

"What was that?" he asked, then turned to Cheryl, "I don't know what she said but it sounded sexy."

"Yeah," Cheryl sighed, "let me help you."

He gripped her hand. "Man, am I dizzy."

Cheryl grabbed him before he fell. "I got you. We'll take it slow."

***

The last patron stumbled out the door. It was just Susan and Henry the cook.

"Ain't dat someth'n," he said, putting on his coat. "Was anything take'n?" He shook his head. "Nobody's safe nowhere."

"Jim told me to lock up. You have a good night, Henry."

He gave her a concerned look. "You go'n be alright? Maybe we should call the police?"

After a few seconds' thought, she said no. "Whoever did it…" The image of files strewn all over the floor flashed before her. She was about to say the person was after something else but stopped. Instead, she patted Henry on the shoulder. "*C'est bon*. It is good. I'll be fine. Be careful going home."

She let Henry out and locked the door. The place was eerily quiet. She went behind the bar and found a bottle of Delamain Vesper cognac. She studied the label and decided. This was her payment for being left behind. Expensive and delicious. She reached for a snifter and poured two fingers' worth. The liquid was a deep gold. It was almost too pretty to drink. She took a sip. The cognac warmed her. Her throbbing knee became a bit more bearable.

She emptied the registers behind the bar. *Sacre bleu, there is a shitload of cash*. She counted the money and then dropped it in a large paper bag along with credit card receipts. *Jimmy has a hell of a business*. The evening stash was in the thousands. She flicked off the lights. leaving one on in the back. It was 2:30 in the morning. She wasn't going to the basement and Jim's office without being prepared. She went to her locker and retrieved her purse. She pulled out her Beretta Px4 Storm subcompact pistol and loaded the clip, then flicked off the safety. She would not be a victim a second time.

Chapter Fifty-Nine

Beth nodded to Peter the doorman as he stood by the exit. "Would you be needing a cab, Mrs. Daniels?"

"Thank you but no."

"Is Mr. Daniels all right after that explosion at the Palace?"

Beth drew in a breath. "Yeah, he's fine. He's upstairs resting." She stopped and palmed a $20.00 bill. "Peter, you didn't see me, okay?"

He looked at his hand, then at her. "Whatever you say, Mrs. Daniels. I haven't seen nobody." He opened the door for her. "Have a nice afternoon," he called.

She walked a few blocks, turned slightly to make sure no one had followed, then hailed a cab.

"Where to?"

"LaSalle and Wacker," she said.

"Nice. Going downtown for a little business."

"Uh-huh."

"Well, lawyers cost a ton. My brother-in-law had to see one of them bloodsuckers for a little problem."

"Uh-huh."

"Okay, I get it. You're not interested."

"No offense, I've got a huge headache."

"Sure." He punched the radio and acid rock filled the car.

She closed her eyes and struggled to block out the noise.

The cab weaved through traffic and slowly made its way south.

"Too many cars," the driver said. He could barely be heard.

"Let me out on Hibbard." Her voice leapt over the wailing electric guitars.

He lowered the sound. "What? I thought you said Wacker."

"I was mistaken. There's a Starbucks on the corner."

"No problem. I'll wait."

She tried to be pleasant. "No, this will be fine. It's only a few blocks," and paid the fare. She walked into the store and browsed the menu until she felt enough time had passed. The walk to her destination felt liberating even when the wind caught her on the bridge over the Chicago River.

What is my plan? Joe's secretary? Jesus, I should know her name, but he changed them so often. She reached Joe's building. Across the street, there was yellow tape around the parking lot and several cops and cars blocking the entrance.

The security guard greeted her.

"Why, Ms. Daniels, how is Joe?"

"He's doing better, thank you."

He punched in her name and produced her pass. "Here you are. Please tell Joe hello."

"Sure will." Her promise felt as false as the smile on her face.

***

The elevator door opened on the twenty-seventh floor to the waiting area of the law firm. Behind the rich mahogany reception desk, the firm's name appeared on the wall in large gold letters. Her husbands' was at the end. The large, thick, Oriental rug on the polished wood floor signaled *this was going to cost* to the supplicants of their services.

"May I help you?" the twenty-something girl dressed in a woman's professional suit asked.

Beth suppressed the indignity that she was not known

and bit her lip. "Yes, I'm Mr. Daniels' wife. He asked me to pick something up from his office."

The girl's eyes opened wider. "Oh, I'm...I'm so sorry. I mean I didn't expect, I mean..."

"That's okay, just buzz me in."

Chapter Sixty

The phone startled Joe awake. The last thing he remembered was Beth had drawn the curtains and shades. As he searched for the ringing instrument, he noticed the blankets were scattered.

At first, the caller was difficult to understand. He had a heavy accent. Then the person said "girlfriend" and the darkness parted into a searing vision of Nicole. The bastard wouldn't give him any information, only…something about guns. He took a breath. His sides hurt. He leaned forward and rubbed his forehead with the phone. Nicole. "*She was doing what she does best,*" were the caller's words. *What the hell did that mean? What does she know about his gun-running? Jesus, this is out of hand.*

The conversation had ended suddenly. *Maybe I dreamt it.* He checked 'recent calls'. 'Unknown' stared back at him. *Shit.* It was real.

"Beth," he called. "Beth?" *Too much to wish for.* He moved to the edge of the bed and waited a few seconds to collect his strength and thoughts. Then he put his feet on the carpeted floor and carefully moved toward the bedroom entrance.

He opened the door and called, "Are you here?" No answer. He went down the hallway. Her wine glass along with a bottle rested by the chair near the living room window. "Beth?"

Steam rose from the lake. He rubbed his arms and a cold chill ran through his body. The memory of the freezing night was very fresh. *Where the hell is she? But why worry about her. Nicole, kidnapped?* He took a few steps toward the bathroom and stopped. *Blackmail.* The word hit him like a fist to his gut. *That's what all of this is about. "She was doing what she does best."* He came back to that phrase. *Is Nicole part of this scheme or a victim?* It didn't matter now. Someone was out to get him.

***

Joe left the apartment.

"Mr. Daniels, so nice to see you," Peter the doorman said.

The words stopped Daniels. "You see me every day, Peter."

The doorman's smile vanished. "I eh, I mean, after the other night and the police and all."

"Police?"

"Didn't Mrs. Daniels tell you?"

"Tell me what?"

The doorman edged toward the front door and opened it. "None of my business, sir. I'm just glad everyone is okay."

Daniels put on his hat and gloves. "I don't know what you're talking about." He took a step. "Have you seen my wife today?"

Peter held the door. "No, sir," he hesitated. "I got a late start."

"You positive?"

"Uhm, sure am. I know your wife. Haven't seen her."

"All right, Peter, we'll talk about this later."

***

Daniels sat at a table with his back toward the door. Even in his ritzy neighborhood there was always a spot for an everyday kind of place. June, that was his street name, sat across from him.

"You look worse dan dem street beggars," June said with a laugh. "Hey you," he called to a waitress, "hey baby, uhm, you be like butter on bread." He flipped his coffee cup. "I needs some."

Daniels forced himself to be patient. June was a former client who knew the streets well. "Hey, don't do that. I'm a regular here." He smiled in the hope the waitress, Clara, wouldn't be angry by his ill-mannered companion. "My friend here would like coffee," he said.

"Yo, I speaks English. Da bitch knows what I'z want. Don't you?" June 's large face had a menacing look.

The young shapely Hispanic waitress poured the coffee.

"See, she know. Baby you could warm up my night anytime."

"Will there be anything else, Mr. Daniels?" she asked.

"Enough, June. You want something to eat?"

"She know you. D-a-m-n! You too uptight, man. I'm jest play'n. Don't mean anything by it." He gave the waitress a look. "But I'm always interested." He glanced at the menu. "Give me a hamburger with everything."

Joe braced himself for the next question. He stared at June.

"How would you like that cooked?" she asked.

June's grin went from ear to ear. "Baby, I likes my meat pink, if you knows what I mean."

"Jesus," Joe said under his breath. He pointed at a menu item. "A salad for me. Ranch on the side."

"Thank you," but she lingered a second or two before moving from the table.

Chapter Sixty-One

"Allo, allo?" Jack Monte spoke into his phone. There was no French or Canadian accent. "Ivan, are you there? God damn it."

The call went into voicemail. "Leave message, busy."

Monte rubbed his knuckles while listening. He swore in Serbian, then said, "I found Dumond's associate. Call me back."

He could see his breath in the night's air as he put distance between the bar and himself. He slipped the phone back into his pocket. *Damn Ivan. What the hell is he doing?* But Ivan was always doing. Women, booze, guns, the son-of-a-bitch was perpetually in motion. He carefully looked over his shoulder. When he saw nothing alarming, he slowed down. A tourist on a stroll. It was dumb of him to search the office for the bitch's address. He should have anticipated an intrusion. It was the booze. No clear head or was it his dick talking. *I should have waited for her call. She would have called, given the look on her face when I used Dumond's name. Now Ivan is needed.*

He climbed the stairs leading to the El which ran by the Merchandise Mart. There was a crowd of twenty-somethings gathered on the platform. The wait wasn't long. The train pulled in and the people, some on their phones, others laughing, surged into the various cars. He found a seat next to a large woman whose head leaned on the window. *No need for conversation.* He glanced at the nothingness of the outside. It was the same blackness of the ambulance that had carried Dumond after he was shot in Paris. He was the paramedic on the scene and played that part well. By the time they'd arrived at the hospital, Dumond no longer had his phone, keys, or papers. A few words to the emergency room doctors and Monte vanished. A magician who'd perfected the art of disappearing. In France, he was Sergey, in England, Alan, only a very few knew his real name. It was his idea to get rid of Dumond. Why deal with the middle-man? His organization had learned that Dumond had a contact in the States by monitoring his phone. *Voila*, Susan. He just didn't know she was also beautiful.

The train lurched into a station whose name could barely be read. The loudspeaker announced Fullerton. The next stop was his.

Chapter Sixty-Two

Nicole's arms hurt as she pointed the gun at Ivan's head. "Tell me, you scum. Where are we? Are more of your bastard friends coming?"

"So many questions. *Tsk tsk*, you are so beautiful." His hand went to his zipper. "I'd get it out of my pants but it's difficult…" He looked at her, his eyes sharp. "Water," his voice cracked, "so I will have strength." He pointed to a faucet. "Please."

"Shut up. Answer my questions and I'll get it."

"You learn quick. You are now the master of my game."

"Never. We are not the same."

A cough cut off his laugh. He put his left hand over his wound. He swallowed and in a gravelly voice said, "You don't think so…eh? I use what I have to get what I want. So do you."

"Keep talking and I'll shoot you again."

"You will anyway. But we do have a difference."

"Yeah? What's that?"

"I do these things for a cause. You do it for yourself."

"You piece of shit. You justify murder and slavery in the name of Serbia. You only wrap your evil in words you have contempt for, like freedom. For who? Assholes like you?"

A smile crossed his face. "You gave Georgie a good time. He died a happy man. I want to go out like him. It's my dying wish." He pointed to his pants zipper.

"Fuck you," she said in Serbian. Her finger tightened around the trigger and the gun went off.

The bang of the weapon startled her. The gun fell. She stood frozen and stared at Ivan's forehead. Blood gushed out the back of his head, splattering the wall. *He's dead.* The thought fluttered inside her brain. *He's dead. I murdered him. I…I…*

She ran to the bathroom and threw up, then stumbled to the sink. The mirror reflected a face streaked with tears and droplets of blood all over her body. "No," she screamed. "Ivan's blood…no." She grabbed a wash cloth and soaked it in water. She dabbed the cloth all over her in a frenzy motion. The coldness against her skin made her tremble. Her teeth chattered. The ring of a telephone came from the next room where the bodies were. *Oh God.* Her heart raced. *Should I answer? What if more of those bastards are on their way?* She struggled to keep from crying. Her legs gave out and she sank to the floor. She buried her head in her arms and between sobs gasped for air. *There is no future. More of those animals will come and after fucking me, if that's all they will do, I'll be killed, or sold or… Stop.* She looked up. Nothing had changed. She was in the bathroom…alone but alive. She had to get away. She pulled herself up by using the sink as support.

She wobbled and went back into the bedroom. The phone had stopped. She retrieved the towels that Georgie had taken off her and wrapped herself. Then she took a deep breath. Her hand shook as she strained to avoid Ivan's bloody face. She touched his coat. The leather was rough. She ran her hand down the lapel and then into one of the front pockets. It was empty. She glanced at the coat and then searched a zippered hidden compartment. She grasped something hard and pulled it out. In her bloody hand was the phone. She brought it to her face and saw there was a missed call. She looked around the room and took a step to where she had dropped the gun. She'd be ready for whoever comes.

Chapter Sixty-Three

"Of all the places we could have grabbed a bite, this is the one you chose?" Billy Dee asked. "This neighborhood has the best of everything, but you, Shep, the connoisseur of food, pick a joint that's in any neighborhood in Chicago."

"Are you done?" Shep said, shutting off the car. "I like this place. It's cheap, good food, good service, and the coffee is great. To me, it's a no-brainer."

They entered the restaurant which was a few blocks from Mr. Daniels' apartment. They were met by a middle-aged hostess who wore bright red lipstick and heavy eyeshadow.

"Gentlemen, do you prefer a booth or a table?"

"Booth," Billy Dee said.

"Table," Shep answered.

"Really?" Billy Dee stared at his friend.

"All right, booth."

They were given a spot at the front which provided a view of the street as well as those in the restaurant. She left menus on the table.

"Do either of you care for a paper? *Sun-Times* or *Trib?*"

"*Sun-Times*, I want to check the scores and the time of the Bulls game," Billy Dee said.

"Jesus, don't you have a phone to do that?"

"I like reading about it."

The hostess returned with a newspaper for each.

"Comfy," Shep asked.

Billy Dee flipped the paper to the front page. "Yeah, what's good here?"

Shep took a second. "Everything has just the right amount of grease. Can't go wrong with eggs or their BLT sandwich with extra mayo."

"Good to know," and went back to skimming the paper. The place was bustling, with a steady hum of conversations occasionally interrupted by a baby's cry.

"Hey, look on page three." The article was continued from page 1, with a picture of Joseph Daniels as one of the victims of the Palace parking lot bomb.

"What does it say?" Shep asked.

"You got a paper."

"Yeah, but you're there already."

Billy Dee looked up, eyed his partner and went back to the story. "It says 'he was discharged from the hospital and that his injuries weren't severe.' According to the paper, Daniels made no statement as to who could have been behind the bombing or whether he was the target. Chicago Police stated 'they were investigating.'"

"Can always count on the media to get it right," Shep said, then sipped his coffee. "Bullshit. You know what this means?"

"What?"

"The police got nothing. No fucking idea what happened at that garage."

"Hold on, maybe for once we're being smart and keeping our yaps shut."

"For what?"

"Until it all comes together. Forensics most likely is trying to figure out the device and we need to talk to Joe Daniels."

"Are you ready to order?" the young Hispanic waitress, Clara, asked.

Billy Dee looked up. "How long have you been standing there?"

"Not long. I'll come back if you're not ready."

"No, that's okay. I'll have the BLT, light on the mayo."

"And you'll have the usual?"

"Yeah, but with extra mayo."

"Thank you." She finished jotting down the requests and turned to leave. "Excuse me." Her face took on color. "I couldn't help overhear, but Joe Daniels is sitting near the back with that other gentleman. He too is a regular."

Chapter Sixty-Four

The street racket below the Belmont stop floated up to the train platform. Even though it was close to 2:30 a.m., the lights from the various taverns were on and the music boomed. Cars sped along the road, horns blaring. Jack Monte made his way down the stairs to street level. He was pissed. Ivan hadn't returned his call and Susan…*damn the bitch. Calm down,* he told himself. *This is how mistakes are made.* It was too bad he was interrupted going through the files. *The office was a disorganized mess. Couldn't find a thing. Personnel information was on bits of paper. A name here, a phone number there. Who runs a business like that?* "Fuck," he said loudly in Serbian. Passersby glanced at him and continued their way. *Whoever I hit in that office is lucky to be alive. I would have finished him off but… damn, such is luck. It smiles by opening a door and then slams it in your face.* He got to the corner of Belmont and Seminary and waited for the light to change.

"Hey, you look'n for fun?" a blond-haired early twenties male dressed in a thin jacket and wearing a baseball cap asked. He stood near a street light pole at least twenty feet from Jack.

"What was that?"

The man took a step closer. "You want some action?"

I should keep walking. The man was skinny and dressed too thinly. There was a tattoo on his neck. He looked like a walking advertisement for HIV.

Instead, Jack asked, "What kind of action?"

The twenty-something smiled. "A good time."

Jack gave the impression that he was thinking about the offer. "With you?"

The young man nodded. "Yeah, and I've got some good shit at my crib. It will be worth your while."

"How much?"

There was no hesitation. "A C note gets the party going."

"Where?"

He pointed to a building one in from the corner—Hotel Belmont.

Jack's hands itched as his anger on the inside rose. "Lead the way."

"Not so fast. Where's the green?"

"Let's get out of the light. Over there." Jack pointed.

The twenty-something went to the darkened spot between the corner building. "Okay, we're good."

Jack made a motion of reaching into his pocket but instead punched the twenty-something in the stomach, and as he doubled over, landed another fist on his face. The man fell to the ground. Jack went through his pockets and took the money he had. "You fuck'n queer," he said, "you get what you deserve."

Jack straightened up and looked to see if anyone had noticed. Behind him, the kid moaned. He turned and kicked him. "Shut up," and walked away, his thoughts now clear. He would find Susan with or without Ivan's help.

Chapter Sixty-Five

Beth walked through the office and glanced at the secretaries in their cubicles, wondering which one Joe was sleeping with. *Not her, she's too tall. That one, too small on top.* Another walked by—*nope, too big in the ass.* She reached Joe's corner office and had her hand on the doorknob.

"Excuse me, can I help you?"

The distinctive Bostonian accent stopped her. She turned—Joe's secretary.

"Joanie, how are you?" she said.

"Oh, Mrs. Daniels. I didn't… How's Mr. Daniels? The paper said his injuries were not all that severe. I tried calling several times, but there was no answer."

"He's resting. He asked me to get a file from his office."

"I would have been happy to. You didn't have to come down here."

"It's quite all right. You can only watch a sleeping man for so long."

They laughed.

"Men are such babies. They get a scratch and it's the end of the world."

"That's all that happened? He's very lucky. The pictures made it seem a lot worse."

"Newspapers," Beth said.

"If you need help, I'll be around the corner. Another one of our attorneys didn't make it in today and hasn't been heard from."

"Huh. That's unusual. Joe says he runs a tight ship."

Joanie smiled. "He does. She's new. Maybe she's working on a project for Mr. Daniels that she forgot to tell us about."

"Should I let Joe know when I get back home?"

"No, no, I'm sure Nicole has a reason. No need to disturb your husband."

"Okay. Thanks, Joanie. Nice chatting with you. I'll only be a minute or two." Beth closed Joe's office door behind her. *Nicole must be the bitch he's playing around with. Secret project … you betcha it's secret.* She sat down on Joe's high-back chair and surveyed his desk. He kept it clean…too clean, as if no one worked there. She bent toward the floor and got the desk keys from her purse. She had made a copy long ago. Knowledge, as is said, is power and learning Joe's vulnerabilities kept her a few steps ahead.

Chapter Sixty-Six

Joe tried to get June to stay on subject, but it was like herding rabbits. "What do you hear on the street?"

June smiled broadly. "What's you wants to know. Da man crack'n heads in the hood. Can't run a game no how. Pills, pussy, don't matter, the man wants some…"

"June, I'm not asking about that."

"You ain't?" He picked up his cup and slurped. He looked dumbfounded. "Then wha'cha ask'n?"

Joe leaned across the table. "The word on the street. What the hell are Bug and Drey up to, dumb shit."

June looked away. "Where be dat mighty fine waitress. Uhm hum. Fuck the food, I'll just grab her. Whatcha think?"

Joe turned for a second and then back to him. "What?"

"I'm go'in to make her feel sooo good." He started to get up.

"Sit down, damn it, and get your mind off that shit." His patience was close to walking. "I need information. Bug, Drey?"

"All right, all right. I hear you. Don't go all up in my face. I'm ragg'n you a bit."

Joe leaned back in his chair and waited. "Well?"

"Can't talk on an empty stomach. Man gots to eat."

"Shit. You listen good. I got you out of more jams than most people have in several lifetimes. Those bastards tried to kill me last night. I need to know what is going on."

"You're look'n serious, man."

"That's what happens when death is real possible."

"Okay, gotcha. Just have'n eyes see you and me ain't good for my health, but you be my amigo."

Joe absently played with his fork.

"Here's the thing…straight. Drey …."

The Hispanic waitress, Clara appeared with their orders. "You had the burger?" she said to June. "Pink is how you wanted it?"

"Uh-huh." He didn't look up.

"And for you, Mr. Daniels, I have a salad with ranch dressing. Will there be anything else?"

June looked up from his plate. "The burger done good, just like your… hey." June dropped the bun.

"What now?"

"Dere's two guys stare'n at us."

"Where?" Joe asked.

"Up there. Do you know them?"

Joe turned to gaze, where June indicated.

"That's Detective Sheppard," Clara said, "He wants to talk to you. I'm waiting on his table." She paused, "and while taking their order I overheard some of the conversation.

Chapter Sixty-Seven

Susan put the money in the safe and closed it. Then she inspected several of the files that were strewn on the floor. Most were of personnel. Jimmy must have a high turnover rate. She did not find hers. *Assez de temps perdu. Enough wasting time.* She unlocked the back door and turned off all the lights except a lamp in Jimmy's office. Then she found a hiding place with a clear view of the back exit. Her gun rested in her hands. The wait stretched into an hour. The cognac she'd had earlier made her drowsy. She'd close her eyes, then wake with a start. She thought of going to the bathroom and splashing water on her face, but that required movement, which her body was against. Doubt began to seep in. *He'd be a fool to return. A trained operative would not do that. But this Jacque Monte or whatever he called himself wasn't that smart. Arrogant, yes. Doesn't need to think because of his looks. His French was nonsense—grade school at best. But who else would have done this? It was him.* She went back and forth, making arguments to stay awake. But she ran out of theories. Her body demanded sleep. Her eyes closed and the night sounds of the place vanished.

***

She was on a bench in the Tuileries Garden. It must have been spring because the air was expectant and the buds on the trees were about to burst. Lovers walked arm in arm. He

187

told her to be there at eleven and now it was close to noon. She hated to wait, and he knew that, which made her angry. She looked at her watch, then stood. *Merde.* Then she saw him. He strolled along. It seemed he took in everything around him. He was dressed in a long wool coat with a scarf around his neck and carried flowers.

"*Pour toi*," he said. "I'm sorry I am late."

"Dumond." She opened her mouth to voice her anger, but the smell and beauty of the roses swept her. "*Bon, merci.*" She could feel her face glow.

"You forgive me?"

She paused. "*Certainement*. How can I not?"

"*Bon*. Let's walk."

She put her hand in his; they went down gravel paths. "About the guns," he said.

***

Jack Monte hadn't expected it to be so easy. He drove past the restaurant/bar and saw it was dark. Then he pulled into the alley. He drove an old white van that had small windows on the side doors. The word *MEAT* was scrolled across the side. He cut the lights and motor and checked his phone. Neither Ivan nor Susan had called. He had to find her, and time was short. He hopped out. The long coat he wore was weighted down by the gun in his pocket. A rag soaked in ether was in his gloved hand. He looked down the alley for signs of anyone. Then he went to the curb. The street was quiet, as it should be at 3:30 a.m. Satisfied that the area was clear, he went down the two steps that led to the back exit. At this hour, he would have the time to find her information or... He put his hand on the doorknob and gave a slight twist. *Shit, it isn't locked.* He thought about what that meant. *Carelessness? Or is she or someone else waiting for him? I could leave.* He took a small step away from the door. He felt his hands sweat. *Why hasn't Ivan called? Surprise your enemy, is his motto. No one would expect me to return, therefore, it is an oversight the door is unlocked.* He stepped forward and tried the handle again. *One-two-three.*

He burst in and saw her asleep in the corner. Two quick strides and he was upon her, rag in hand. He forced the cloth over her face, covering her nose and mouth. She twisted her body and grunted. Her arms clawed the air but he had superior strength and within a minute or two, the struggle stopped He removed the towel, then stooped and picked up her gun and purse. The weapon must have fallen from her lap. He studied the pistol in an acknowledgment that his scheme could have ended differently. He did a cursory search of the basement and then went to the van and retrieved tape, rope, and a large canvas tarp.

He tied her hands and feet. The tape went over her mouth. Then he threw the tarp over her and carried her out like a slab of beef. Instead of a trunk there was the compartment for a bench seat that was already elevated. He rolled her off the sheet and into the vacated space. He snapped the compartment shut and closed the rear door. The operation took five minutes.

***

She felt gravity push her as if she was in a car that made a turn. It woke her. It was dark. Her arms and legs were bound and there was something covering her mouth. She heard wind whistling above and felt bumps. She must be in a trunk? *Mon Dieu.* Her breathing was too fast as she tried to remember. *How did I get here?* She had fallen asleep. She awoke because light came through the open back door. He was upon her in an instant. Her gun must have fallen.

The son of a bitch grabbed her face. The last thing she remembered was a chemical smell. Was there only him or did he have help? She forced herself not to shake, but shuddered anyway. *Dumond, where the fuck are you? You plan for everything. Was this included?* She breathed deeply to calm herself. She had lived her life by her wits and looks; that was why Dumond had chosen her. Those could not fail her now.

She felt the vehicle sway and heard the crunch of gravel under the tires. She didn't know how long she'd been confined, but her bladder told her it had been a while. *Que diable? What the fuck?* She lay on her side, her bruised knees drawn up in a semi-fetal position. She tried to stretch but her feet struck the wall of the space. The upper portion of her body rested on the bottom of the compartment. With every bump, her shoulder grazed the lid. If she strained, she could see or maybe imagined light around what she thought was a seam above her. Given the dimensions, she figured she was not stowed in a trunk, unless the vehicle was very small. She listened. The motor whined and gears shifted. She peered upward and prayed it was indeed light. With all the force she could manage, she struck the top with her shoulder. On the fourth attempt a latch gave way, and she felt air. She wiggled herself to a sitting position. She was in a van with a back- door inches from her. A bench seat was on the other side.

Chapter Sixty-Eight

Which locked drawer held that fuck'n file? His desk had four of them and then there was his credenza. Beth inserted the key into the top left one. *Click.* With a slight pull, it opened. There were papers on top of each other along with bank statements, subpoenas, and bills. She grabbed a pile. An envelope fell. Allerton Hotel? She picked it up and withdrew the statement. *That little fucker. That's his pied-à-terre.* She studied the dates. Now she knew where he went when he "worked late" and had a good idea with whom. *So, he was getting some while she did the same.* She closed her eyes for a second or so. *Ah, Sonny or Anatoly, you were so…* She sighed and sifted through the rest of the papers. Within minutes, she found nothing more of interest and dumped the pile back in the drawer. She studied the desk, then swiveled in her chair and eyed the credenza. *Maybe in there.* She used another key. The cabinet door opened. *Jesus, what a mess.* Files were stuffed haphazardly in the space. *How does that man work?* She bent over and grabbed a few.

"Find what you were looking for?" Joanie asked.

Beth dropped the pile she held as she didn't hear her come in. "Oh."

"I'm so sorry. I must have startled you?"

"No—well yes. I'm trying to remember which file Joe asked me to find. He wasn't all that coherent and I foolishly didn't write it down."

"Let me help you pick them up."

"Don't be silly. It's not a problem. He told me the name, and I'll recognize it when I see it." She knelt on the carpet to gather the pile.

Joanie didn't look convinced. "I know Joe is resting, but you could be here a long time. I'm sure he'd be okay if you called."

Beth got off her knees and straightened. "No…not a good idea. I'll figure it out."

"Well, Ms. Daniels, because of privacy laws and all that, I'm sure you understand, you can't rummage through every file."

"Uh-huh. I'll just be another minute…really. If it's not in here I'll leave and have Joe call."

Joanie took a step toward her. "I'm sorry, but I can't…"

Beth knew she was losing the argument. She glanced down. "Wait, there it is. That's the one he wanted." She pointed.

"Which one?"

Beth stooped and grabbed it. "The Simon file."

"Simon? I don't remember him even working on such a case."

"Really. What can I say? Men—they're so mysterious. They expect us to figure out what they don't tell us."

Chapter Sixty-Nine

"A rather large Black guy is giving us the stare," Shep said. "Is he one of yours?"

"Now what the hell do you mean by that?" Billy Dee asked. "Is every white guy who nods one of yours?"

"Don't get so defensive. He's sitting with Daniels."

"Maybe it's brotherhood week. You're sitting with me."

"You're taking it wrong. What I meant was do you recognize the dude from when you ran lock-up?"

Billy Dee put his coffee cup down and looked. "Aren't you glad we're in a booth. I can check this out without being noticed."

"Yeah, yeah, well?"

"I don't think so. He seems more West side business than North. Anyway, they're both eating so they're not going anywhere. Let's have a chat before our food comes."

"Great idea. Both of us?"

"What's wrong with you, man? Has police procedure changed since I left?"

Shep picked up his coffee, took a sip, and put it down. "I, eh, well, what if our food comes while we're talking to them. Damn it, I'm hungry."

"If that don't beat all. There's a basket of bread on the table, take a roll."

Shep didn't move.

"So, what you're say'n is you want me to do the work. Who's carry'n the real badge, for God's sake?"

"I'll back you up by staying put. If either of them tries to leave, I'll have your back."

Billy Dee stopped what he was about to say and shook his head. "Shep, you gett'n to be a piece of work."

"No, listen, I'm not leaving you in the lurch. It's a good plan. I'm the real cop and if something goes south it'll be on me. You can act anyway you want. I can't."

Billy Dee rubbed his chin. "Maybe I've been around you too long, but there's some sense in what your say'n. Damn." He put his napkin on the table and got up.

***

"A brother is coming this way," June said, holding his sandwich in the palm of his huge hand.

"What about the other detective?" asked Joe

"Watch'n."

***

It took Billy Dee several seconds to maneuver between the tables and diners to reach Daniels. "Excuse me, I'm Detective Billy Dee Jackson, CPD, and you must be Joe Daniels."

Daniels continued to eat his salad.

"I'd like a word with you," Billy Dee said.

"Whattabout?"

"The bomb incident at the Palace Garage."

Daniels munched a forkful of lettuce. After swallowing, he gave Jackson a glance, then said, "Give me your card, I'll give you a call." He stabbed a piece of avocado without waiting for a response.

"Mr. Daniels, that's not exactly how it works."

"June, is the detective still here? Doesn't he know it's rude to interrupt someone's dining?"

"Fuck yeah. Mr. Daniels be eating, and don't wants to be bothered," June put down his hamburger and stared.

Billy Dee nodded and stepped behind June. He leaned over the big man. "You be West side business. You don't need to say anything, but we both know." He looked down at the man. "That bulge on your ankle, it's either a bracelet, which means you ain't supposed to be here, or you're pack'n. I'm goi'n to be real nice. Get up slow and join my partner up there. Mr. Daniels and I need to do some talk'n."

Chapter Seventy

Nicole picked up Georgie's coat from the floor. She was swallowed up by the size of the garment, but it was better than wearing mere towels. In his pockets were some Hershey's chocolates that she devoured. The presence of two dead bodies in the room no longer frightened her, though Georgie's large corpse was even more hideous lying face down with his ass in the air. She left the bodies, walked through an adjacent room, and then went up three stairs that led to a kitchen. As she went up the steps, she remembered Ivan shoving her down them. In the eating area there was a window with the shade drawn and dark curtains. The kitchen led into a front room, and a bedroom off to the side. Three windows went across the outer wall. They too were covered. A small amount of light seeped in through the edges. She walked on the wood floor as quietly as she could. Georgie's coat, though, dragged on the surface. Still, she didn't turn on any lights. Even though it was dark, this was someone's house. They could be coming back…or? She approached the bedroom door. *How do they do it on TV?* She hugged the wall and pointed the gun into the room. A nightlight was plugged into an outlet. She saw only a bed. There was a sheet but no bed spread. Only something that appeared to be a blanket. The revolver grew heavy and she lowered her arm.

She reached the front door. She could hear her own breathing. Her hand was on the door knob. Her grip tightened as she raised the revolver with the other. She strained to hear if anyone or anything was on the other side. She slowly turned the handle, then stopped. The window. She left the door and peeked past the edge of the shade. There was little to see as it was night or early morning. There were silhouettes of trees but no street lights. Somewhere along the side of the building there must be a driveway. Ivan had pulled her out of the vehicle and she remembered the garage door closing as he brought her into the house. *Did we go through the front or was there a door by the kitchen?* She stood at the window trying to recall. The music of Ivan's cell interrupted her thoughts. That was the third or fourth call since he was shot. Unanswered phones would bring Ivan's friends. Time was running short. She couldn't stay much longer. She checked Georgie's coat for keys. Not finding any, she went back to the room with the bodies. She stood over the corpses, took a deep breath, and thrust her hand in Georgie's pants that were at his ankles. Nothing. *How the fuck did he get here?* She moved to Ivan. Even though he had been dead for a while, there was a *cat ate the canary* smile on his face. *What secrets does he know? The sonofabitch.* She bent down and tried to avoid the blood on his coat. She put her hand gingerly in his coat pocket. Nothing. She checked the other pocket with the same result. She stood. *Shit.* The keys had to be somewhere. "Where the fuck are they, Ivan?" She almost kicked him out of frustration, then walked around his body. "You're going to make me go through your pants, aren't you? Too bad you won't be able to enjoy it." She stooped again. She put the gun on the floor and reached for his jeans. The noise of a racing car or truck engine came from the front of the house as she touched the material. She jumped and nearly tripped on the coat going up the stairs.

She caught herself and raced to the front window. It was lighter outside. She could see lights and the spray of dust made by something moving fast. The beams became sharper. A white van came into view. It was headed for the house.

Chapter Seventy-One

Billy Dee took June's seat. Joe put down his fork. "Nicely done, detective…?"

"Jackson, Billy Dee Jackson."

"Yes, Detective Jackson. You know, I have a healthy criminal practice, and I don't recall ever running into you."

"This is your lucky day." Billy Dee put both his hands on the table. "Tell me what happened the day of the bombing."

Daniels reached for a glass of water. He must have swallowed wrong as he went into a coughing fit. Then he grabbed his side.

"You okay?" Billy Dee was about to get up.

Daniels wagged a finger, indicating to give him a moment. "I'm… went down the wrong pipe… still hurt from the explosion." He took a minute to compose himself. "Better. Okay." He sat back. "All the years I have been doing this, it's usually me asking the questions or telling my client to shut up. I shouldn't have given you a hard time."

"No apologies necessary. All in a day's work."

"Good."

Billy Dee leaned forward. "You were about to say…"

"Yes, I got in my car, turned the ignition, and that's all I remember."

"What time was that?"

"Jeez, I believe I left the office after six."

"Were you alone?"

"Yes, I'm pretty sure I was the last one out."

"So, no one saw you?"

He shook his head. "I suppose not."

"Do you leave at the same time every day?"

"Not in my business."

Billy Dee smiled, "Same for me. Different day, different time. Anyone pissed off at you?"

Daniels laughed. "Oh, Detective, are you kidding? All clients hate their lawyers."

"Do some hate you more than others?"

Daniels twirled his fork. "Interesting. You think a client could have done it?"

Talking to this guy is like playing chess. Jesus. "I'm only ask'n. You've been on the other side of this business but most of the time, these kinds of things are done by someone the victim knows…business associates, a jealous lover, a wife or husband. The usual bullshit."

"You know your job, Detective. Let me see…" He leaned forward and lowered his voice. "I'm tell'n you this only because you asked, but…" He cleared his throat. "The … eh…wife… and I…" He leaned back and stared at his plate.

"What about your wife?"

"Not so loud, Detective. I'm sure it wasn't her. Don't think she's capable, but we both know people can surprise."

"Your wife? Okay. What's her full name and where can we talk to her?"

"Beth… Beth Daniels, and she lives at the same address… at least for now."

"Got it. Anyone else?"

Daniels turned in his seat and looked in the direction where June and Shep sat. Both were eating. He turned back. "There could be someone. Yes, who knows maybe…?" A quick smile crossed his face.

"Who's that?"

"He's a client so I have to be careful. You didn't get it from me. Understood?"

"Sure."

"His real name is Andre King, but his associates call him Drey."

Chapter Seventy-Two

Beth scooped the Simon file into her oversize handbag. "Thanks, Joanie, I'll tell Joe to call when he wakes."

Joanie didn't move. "You sure that's the file he wanted? I just don't know…" Her smile seemed frozen on her face while she rubbed her hands.

"Honest, it's okay. Blame me if he gives you trouble. I'm only doing what he asked."

"Okay, Ms. Daniels, you know how upset Joe gets when…"

Beth put a hand on her arm. "Believe me, I know." She gave Joanie another affirming pat and walked out of Joe's office. Her gait was steady although her heart thumped so loud she thought everyone in the office heard. But none seemed to have noticed.

The elevator came, she gave a Queen Elizabeth wave, and disappeared behind the sliding doors. She let out her breath. *Simon.* She closed her eyes. This was the file. Her memory clicked. The numerous times Joe received calls at home, whether it was early morning or late at night. His reaction was the same. He'd run down the hall to his office and shut the door. He even did it on the rare occasion when they made love. The damn phone rang and he… She, being curious and pissed, listened by the office door. The one distinct phrase on every occasion was *in the Simon file.*

"Who's Simon?" she'd ask.

His face turned red, and if he answered he'd say, "Not your business and don't mention that name again."

This could be her ticket to freedom and revenge.

The elevator reached the lobby and she stepped out. Her heels echoed on the tiled floor. The security officer wished her a good day and regards to Joe. "Thank you, and of course."

"Can I get you a cab?"

"No, I need the walk."

The blustery November winds made themselves known as she went across the LaSalle Street bridge. She flipped the lapels of her coat to cover the bottom of her face. There was a sandwich place on the corner of Kinzie—a place as good as any. Besides, all of this cloak and dagger activity made her hungry.

She ordered a butternut squash soup and a salad and found an isolated table. There were a few other customers near the front who seemed content to focus on their food. She finished her soup and pulled out the file. A rubberized string wrapped around a paper post kept the file closed. She unwound it and grabbed a fistful of papers.

"What the hell?" she said in a voice that caused those in front to look.

She glared at a legal complaint in which Leo Simon was a defendant. It went on for pages. She looked at the front of the document again. The case number read 1995 L 00438. *How could litigation last twenty-one years?* She grabbed the file again and withdrew several thick manila folders. Each had a label—Service, Answer, Discovery… and toward the back, there were four remaining—Andre King, Bug, Hugo, Anatoly Dmursic. *No, impossible… Sonny?* Her mouth went dry and she reached for a glass of water. Her hand shook and water spilled on the papers. "Shit." There were more stares from the diners.

"Sorry…water…on these documents…" She sopped up the liquid with a napkin. Then rested her hands on the folders. *What was Joe doing and why Sonny?* She closed her eyes and leaned back in the chair, her taste for revenge tempered by a fear of what was inside. *Oh God.*

The sound of a chair's legs scraping the floor made Beth open her eyes and lurch forward. The same large Black man who had come to the apartment in the morning held the chair.

"I'm joining you."

"What? You?"

He ignored her comment. "What's a fine look'n piece do'n eating all by herself with all dese papers?"

"I… "

He reached over to seize the folders.

"What the fuck are you doing? These aren't yours." She grabbed his wrists.

"Bitch. You gots some power in dem hands." He looked directly at her and then at the table. "One of them has my name on it."

"Well, Mr. King, that may be, but they're not yours."

He smiled. "All right…not yet anyways." He let go and sat back.

Neither said anything. Her hands rested on top of the pile of folders as she watched him and he scrutinized her, his stupid grin screwed on his face. Her anxiety grew as the seconds or was it minutes passed.

"Okay, Mr…eh, King or whatever you call yourself. Were you following me? How the hell…?"

He snorted and unbuttoned his coat. "You don't stay alive unless you've got eyes all over."

"The cab driver? Someone in Joe's office. Who?"

"And you don't give up secrets. Just keep them guessing."

"Well, I have no business with you." She picked up a stack of folders and shoveled them into the case file.

"I knows a lot about you," he said.

She paused.

"As I tolds you this morning, Joe's a player. This time a young bitch—great ass, but for me, not enough tits. Not like you. You gots both."

Her arms automatically crossed her chest.

"Whats I'm say'n is Joe disrespects you, as well as me. He don't give a shit for neither one of us. He'd sell us out in a minute."

She thought back to the morning. "Hey, I don't believe a word you're say'n."

"You don't? Why you have dat file? You ain't no lawyer, and I bet my ass dat Joe don't know a thing about it." He leaned a bit forward and placed his large hand on the table. "Think about it. We could fuck up the bastard real good."

Chapter Seventy-Three

"*A*sseyez-vous. *Ne bougez pas* (Sit down. Don't move)," Jack yelled from the driver's seat of the van. "I see what you've done. *Tres bien*, but don't be stupid. *Tu comprends?*"

Susan's hands and feet were still bound and there was tape around her mouth. The very sound of his voice sent a chill through her. She froze. She stared at the vehicle's back door. Then twisted her body to see where he was. Her fear dissipated and gave way to resentment and rage as adrenalin pumped through her. *Keep talking, you* le fils de chien, *I will kill you.*

"I have a gun, *ma petite*, and I'm very good with it. Do what I say. Lie back with your back toward the door."

She didn't move.

"Now."

Her head disappeared behind the rear bench seat.

***

"See, not so difficult. That ass of yours better be kissing the door." He looked to the back one more time, then hopped out and pushed the lock button. He stood outside the van getting his bearings. The morning air was fresh and the sky was clear. There was nothing else around, not a building, a barn, only trees and grass. It took a minute or two to find the gravel path that passed as a driveway. A car was there, but not Ivan's. *Where the fuck is he?* He dialed

Ivan's number and again the call went to voice mail. *That devil. He must be screwing some whore. How the hell did he convince her?* Then he laughed. *The same way Susan got here. Such is their charm. All for the cause.* He went by the parked vehicle to the garage. and punched the code numbers. The door rose and revealed Ivan's van. He touched the engine compartment and it was cold. A few seconds went by, then he walked to the back end and yanked the latch of the rear door. There were dark spots on the floor bed. *Blood?* He slipped his hand into his coat pocket and took out his semi-automatic Beretta.

***

Nicole watched from the corner of the front window as a man stepped out of the white van parked across from the house. She saw him look around as if he wasn't sure where he was. Then he disappeared toward the driveway which was out of view. She tapped Georgie's coat pocket, feeling for the gun. It wasn't there. Her heart thumped against her chest. She checked again, then remembered she put it down near Ivan as she went through his pockets. *Shit. She had to get out.* The front door.

She left her spot by the window and grabbed the door knob. Beads of sweat trickled down her face as she twisted the knob to the left and pulled. Nothing. Her hand shook. She twisted the handle to the right but the door remained shut. She pulled, then pushed while unleashing a string of cuss words, some even in Serbian. Tears mixed with her sweat. She pounded the wood frame. Then took a step back. *It's double locked, fool.* She searched the door for the lock switch. *Oh, Jesus, it's a key…a goddamn key.* She slid down the frame and buried her head in her arms. She rocked back and forth until she heard the distinct sound from the kitchen of a key being inserted.

***

Susan heard him shut the door and step out of the van. She listened to the crunch of his footsteps along the side. Her body tensed as she anticipated him opening the rear door. She held her breath and waited for the click, but it didn't come. There were no sounds at all. *Merde. Where is the bastard? Fuck him.* She lay on her stomach and raised her tied arms behind her back as high as she could. Then slammed them down on her back. After the third time the rope loosened. She twisted her hands until they wriggled free. *No time to deal with the rope burns.* She undid the bindings of her legs and pulled the tape from her mouth. She shook her arms and legs to get circulation, then crawled over the rear bench and crouched behind the driver seat. She slowly moved herself up and peeked out the window. There was only a house. She went to the passenger side and did the same thing—grass and trees. She slipped into the seat, then opened the door and got out. She crawled to the rear of the vehicle and saw a gravel driveway across the way.

Chapter Seventy-Four

"Where can we find this Mr. King?" Billy Dee asked. Joe stretched his arms across the table and turned his palms up. "That's why you're the detective. Investigate. I'm sure somewhere in your department there's a file. I can't give you everything."

"So far, Mr. Daniels, you haven't given us much."

"What do you mean? You now have two suspects. Detective, I didn't see the bastard or whoever planted the bomb. If I did, my car wouldn't have blown up, and I'd be feeling a hell of a lot better."

Two cell phones were on the table and one began to ring.

"Yours or your buddy's?" Billy Dee asked.

Joe looked over and recognized the number. He held up a finger as a sign to wait and picked up the cell.

"Hello. Joanie, what's up? No, I'm ok, a little sore. My wife? Beth did what? I see." He drummed his fingers on the table. "No, I didn't ask her to pick anything up. She took the file? Jesus. What about Nicole? Did you try her mobile? I'll look into it. Bye."

"Bad news?"

Joe didn't answer.

"Hello, Mr. Daniels?"

"What?" He put his phone in his pocket and moved the chair to get up.

"You going somewhere?"

"Sorry, yes, yes I am. We'll have to continue this discussion later." He motioned for June.

"Take my card, actually my partner's, if you think of anything else."

He gave the card a quick look and stuffed in his pocket. Then peeled two twenties from a bundle of cash and left them on the table.

Billy Dee rejoined Shep. "Did you have a nice lunch?" he asked.

"You mean was June a witty conversationalist?"

"Whatever. Hey, where's my food?"

"June. Had to keep him occupied."

"Don't that beat all. At least did you find out anything?"

"In fact, I did. He's the street gossip. Apparently, Mr. Daniels did something that pissed off someone by the name 'Bug'. June didn't know his Christian name-or didn't want to say. He did say Bug is West side."

"That narrows it. He say anything about an Andre King… street name Drey?"

"I'm thinking."

"Write any of this down?"

Shep pointed to his head. "No street files to disclose in discovery. It's all up here."

"Things in your head get lost with all that other information you carry up there."

"Not to worry, Billy Dee, as a matter-of-fact, I remember. June had just devoured his burger and grabbed part of your sandwich. He figured you weren't going to get here any time soon. So, we were bullshitting about crap."

"Uh-huh."

"Then out of the blue he starts talk'n about the hood and places to get fried catfish. Then as he talk'n about food, he drops names of Bug, and I guess your Drey."

"Players or homies?"

"Shit. Before I could pin him down, he left with your man."

Billy Dee sat back and half-listened. He reviewed his own conversation with Daniels. "You know that man accused his wife," he said while Shep talked.

"What?"

"He sure as hell did. Then he gets a phone call and I could see on his face it had something to do with the wife. Whatever she done, Mr. Daniels is hot on her trail. Let's go find Beth Daniels."

"Huh? Where?"

"Their apartment."

"Damn, I haven't finished my coffee."

Chapter Seventy-Five

Jack backed away from Ivan's van and gazed toward the end of the driveway. Not seeing anything unusual, he stepped toward the side door of the house. With one hand he turned the knob and with the other he pointed his gun. The door was locked. *Where the fuck is the key?* He scanned the garage, then looked down at the mat. *Of course, obvious. The old saying keep it simple, stupid.* He bent down, flipped the carpet, and retrieved it. The lock had to be jiggled a bit before the door opened. He stepped in and waited seconds for his eyes to adjust to the darkness. The kitchen blinds were all drawn. A few more steps in, and he heard a noise that came from the front of the house. He trained his gun in that direction and looked. There was a woman dressed in a large coat.

"Don't shoot."

"Come here, slowly, with your hands raised," he said.

The woman walked from the front door. Her hands were over her head, separating the edges of the coat. She stopped a few feet from him. He could see hints of her body.

"What have we here? Are you wearing anything underneath?"

She shook her head.

"What a nice house-warming present. Ivan is thoughtful. Where is he so I can thank him?"

She hesitated, then pointed to the downstairs room.

He took a step or two. "Ivan, was she good? Get up, you sleeping bastard. There's work to do." He looked down the darkened stairs. Then at her. "Come closer." He put his free hand inside the coat and grabbed her tit. "Wow, nice. Ivan," he shouted, "you're too good to me." He motioned for her to take off the garment.

She placed her hands on either side and tried to close the jacket.

"No…off," and pointed the gun at her face.

She let the coat drop to her feet.

He laughed and looked toward the downstairs. "No wonder you didn't answer my calls. You bastard. She must have really tired you out." He took her in with his eyes, then called to Ivan, "The movement can wait. Sometimes a soldier needs a break. Isn't that right." He waited for a response.

When none came, he returned his focus to the naked woman three feet from him. He made a circle with his fingers. "And take your time. It's my turn to enjoy."

She turned her torso slowly but watched him.

"Your head too." He touched the small of her back. Then ran his finger down the crack of her ass.

"Bend."

He touched her. "Hmm, maybe you are also tired. You're not wet. Too bad," he said while rubbing, "but if you don't get hot, you are here for us to enjoy." He grabbed around her waist and pushed her toward the stairs. "I am counting on as good a time as Ivan's."

"Sure. I'll give you a great fuck." Her voice was low and sexy. "There's another bedroom off to the side," she pointed. "There will be more room as there's only one bed down there and…"

"Of course. Ivan needs his rest."

***

Susan had crawled on her belly up the driveway and the

gravel bit into her clothes. She saw Jack at the foot of the garage turn and look in her direction. *Does the bastard see me?* She took cover and crouched behind the parked vehicle and wished there was a hole to dive into. She heard no sound other than the gentle breeze and the sway of tree limbs. Her weight rested on her haunches. Her thigh muscles ached as well as her knee. There was no way to judge how much time passed, but her body urged her to do something.

She snuck along the back bumper of the vehicle and looked. The son of a bitch left the garage door open. She stayed low to the ground and quickly strode the seventy-five feet. She got to the back of the van parked there and caught her breath. The van's rear door was open. She carefully navigated the back of the vehicle and looked in. There were dark spots that appeared to be blood on the floor bed. *Who are these people?* She glanced from that interior to a door on the side of the building. *He must have gone into the house.* She straightened and moved alongside the vehicle looking for anything that could be used as a weapon. A screwdriver and medium sized hammer hung on a peg board fastened to the front wall. *They will have to do.* She put the screwdriver under her sleeve with the blade pointed out and tucked the hammer in her belt.

***

Jack held onto her waist as she led him to the bedroom. The room's furniture consisted only of a bed. He shoved her into a corner and told her not to move. He undid the sheet and felt the mattress. "Can never be too careful." His hand rested on the bed. "Now, come here." A few seconds passed. "I said come here." He raised his gun.

She went to him.

"Lie down." He stood over her. "Ivan certainly has an

eye for beauty." His finger grazed her lips. "I too can pick beautiful women."

"I'm sure you can." She lay with her legs tightly together, her arms by her side.

He sat down next to her. He watched the rhythm of her breathing as he ran his hand down her neck and then to her tits. "See, you are getting aroused. This will be good for both of us."

He continued massaging her nipple. "Yes, the bitch I brought is quite nice. Maybe you will meet her after we're done. Ivan can try her, then…who knows, we all party."

"That would be fun. Where is your friend…I mean, bitch. Don't you want two women at once?"

His hand went between her legs. Her eyes closed. He felt her getting moist and breathing more rapidly. "Ach, my bitch isn't going anywhere. She is safe where she is." He withdrew his hand. "Turn over. Lie on your stomach with your head straight."

"What happened? I've obeyed and done what you asked. What about the other…"

"Do it and stop talking."

He stared at this female form, her hair draped over slim shoulders and down her shapely back. The curve of her hips accentuated her rounded ass that connected to beautifully formed legs. He actually salivated. "My bitch can wait. I want you for myself." He undid his belt and took off his pants. "Now we play."

Chapter Seventy-Six

Beth stared at her uninvited guest. "What's in it for you? Aren't you my husband's client… Mr. King?"

"Here de thing, your man fucked up big time with a few of my associates. Dis ain't the first time. Now as a businessman, dere's always loss, but if it goes on, what happens?" He sat back and waited.

"You go bankrupt? Get killed? I don't know. What kind of business are you in."

"You get the idea."

She shook her head, "No, I really don't. What's in this file that helps you?"

"If I'm right, dem papers have dates, suppliers, customers, and sticks your old man sold."

"Drugs? Joe sold fuck'n drugs? He didn't make enough from his practice that he had to sell dope. Jesus."

It was King's turn to shake his head. "No, he didn't do drugs. He did guns."

"What? Joe's a goddamn gun runner? My God, Jesus, Mary, and Joseph. I always thought Joe was slimy but this…? I can't believe."

"Check it out. I bet it all be there."

She looked from him to the legal file on her lap. "I don't know. This isn't the place. Too many people around."

"What? Girl. Dose people are stuff'n their faces. They could give two shits."

"Well?" She took a deep breath then ran her hand through her hair. I don't know. Damn, if the government knew… oh my God."

"You gots that right. His ass wouldn't see daylight for a long time."

"But you'd go down too."

"Maybe."

"Huh?"

"Who say we go to the goddamn government? The threat be good enough. I gets what I want and so do you. Besides, nothing says we can't edit. Certain papers could…hmm, disappear. You know what I'm talk'n about."

She tried to judge whether this… street… er… gang leader? could be trusted. Even though he came off tough and threatening, there was something smart about him, and in an odd way, believable. She played with the string that tied the file.

"Looky here," he said, "you runn'n on hate. Ain't dat right?"

"I..er…"

"Come on, you wouldn't be here if you weren't. Don't fuck with me. We knows someone already took a crack at him in the parking lot." He lowered his gaze and paused.

"You mean the bombing?"

"Don't play dumb."

She let his comment sink in. "Wait a goddamn minute. I do hate him, but … no way. I don't know anything about that. Make a bomb? You must be joking. Where the fuck would I get…"

He leaned in. "Lower your voice. You want the whole damn place to hear you?"

"You're pissing me off." She put her hand into the sleeve of her coat. "I'm…"

"The sonofabitch fucks anything in sight, ring or no ring." He went on. "To me it's business … an opportunity. We be on de same side of the street. When youz gots a door open, don't mess up. It don't stay dat way forever."

"What do you mean? I have the file." She took her coat off.

"You sure do. Where you goin' to put it. Your crib?"

"Shit." She looked across the table. At least he didn't gloat. He won for now. "Okay, I'll give you the file, but not here. Let's go where some of this can be copied."

Chapter Seventy-Seven

"Your phone is going off," Billy Dee said.

"I hear it, but I'm driving, Goddammit. Some asshole brother of a cop probably stops us and writes me a ticket."

"Aren't we a band of blue?"

Shep made a face. "Yeah right. Things ain't what they use to be."

"Then I'll answer. Give me the damn cell."

Shep fished in his pocket. He found it after the call went dead. "Hey sorry. It takes me awhile. Who was it?"

"No name, just a number starting with 312."

"It's either a robo-call or someone real. Call back. Let's take a chance."

"No problem." Billy Dee pressed to repeat the number. "It's ringing. Hello?"

A male voice answered. "Yes? Who's this?"

"You called a minute ago," Billy Dee answered. You dialed Detective Sheppard's number. Can I help you?"

"Sheppard? I was looking for Detective Jackson."

"Speaking."

"Huh?"

"Is this Mr. Daniels? I gave you Sheppard's number, and I'm answering his phone."

"What? Okay, whatever." Static came over the line from Daniels' breathing. "You claimed I didn't give you much information, well, I, eh, I think my wife may really be involved. What I said to you at the restaurant was a hunch, but now I'm thinking, she really had something to do with the bombing."

"Yeah? Why?" Billy Dee covered the phone and turned to Shep. "Give me some paper."

Shep pointed at the clip board hanging from the dash.

Billy Dee grabbed it. "You there, Mr. Daniels?"

"Of course."

"So, what information do you have?"

"This isn't easy for me, but I think, no, I'm sure my wife is having an affair. She thinks I don't know she bought an apartment a few months ago. It's in the south loop. She's fucking some guy named Dmursk."

"Can you spell it?"

"Jesus, D-m-u-r-s-k, something like that."

"What's his first name?"

"Antoine, Anat, I don't know."

"What about this Dmursic?"

"When I believed my wife was cheating, I did some digging. This guy Dmursic was hooked up or affiliated with an organization."

"Go on."

"Called the Serbian something front, I don't recall exactly. But what I found out is this group blows things up."

"In this country or over there."

"Shit, what's the difference? He's a terrorist sonofabitch."

"Where did you get this information, Mr. Daniels?"

"Detective, you're not the only ones who investigate. Anyway, I believe my wife is somewhere downtown, maybe near my office."

"Really? Was that the phone call?"

There was a pause. "Yes."

"Can you be more specific? And do you have a photograph?"

"My guess is she's heading home from LaSalle and Wacker Drive. Try north of the river and I'll text you one."

"Thanks."

Chapter Seventy-Eight

Nicole struggled to stay composed. Whether he fucked her or not didn't matter as long as she survived. The only plan left was to tire him out, then grab his gun. She endured his breath on her face, but then his hand traced an imaginary line from the nape of her neck down to the small of her back. His touch sent tiny sensations that grew and soon overpowered the fear. He gently parted her legs and she felt his tongue between them. Despite the threat that death loomed close, she squirmed and let out a soft moan that surprised her. She let go and drifted to a sensory high. She wasn't in that room or in that house. There weren't two dead bodies in the lower room. There was clear fresh air and an endless blue sky. Her body exhilarated. The angst left behind. She saw herself flying, ascending into pleasure, then suddenly there was an onrush of pain. It took a second or two for her to realize he had smacked her ass. She opened her eyes from the sharpness of the slap and saw him standing by her head. The gun in his hand.

"Turn this way." He motioned.

She went on her side.

"If you do anything that causes me pain, it will be the last thing you do."

He was large as he forced his dick into her mouth. His free hand firmly grasped the back of her head.

She choked and he let go.

"It will be better if you…" she caught her breath, "let me do it myself."

He looked at her and after a moment said, "Okay," and pointed the gun at her head. "Do it."

She took him into her mouth and it didn't take long for him to moan. His breathing accelerated. He gasped when she cupped his balls.

"Okay," his chest heaved. He motioned her to move and he laid down, then pointed that she should be on top.

He had one hand around her waist; the other loosely gripped the gun. She maneuvered herself over him and guided his entry. Then she rocked her body. He grabbed her tit and forced her to lie over him. Her nipple in his mouth interrupted his grunts.

***

Susan twisted the knob of the side door. The dumb shit Jack never relocked it. She found the kitchen to be dark and waited a few seconds for her eyes to adjust. Moaning sounds and the distinct squeak of bed springs came from the front of the house. *Is this some kind of whorehouse? Why would he bring me here?* She continued to listen. *The bastard must be in that room.* She slipped the hammer from her belt and moved past the stairs. She glanced down into the darkness and, not hearing anything, moved slowly toward the front.

Chapter Seventy-Nine

"Now how are we going to find this woman?" Shep asked. "She could be anywhere. Do we even know she's walking? She could be in a cab or Uber. This isn't exactly strolling weather." Shep turned the vehicle around and travelled south on LaSalle Street.

"Blah, blah. Come on, man, Daniels may be full of crap but this adds a new twist. This Dmursic may be the key and Daniels' wife would know."

"Hold on, I've got a thought."

Billy Dee saw he was serious.

"You think this is that prick's homicide, Detective O'Brien?"

"Let me think on that." Billy Dee took out a cigar but didn't light it. "Could be. Yeah, good reason why we couldn't interview her. But somewhere along the line, O'Brien let her go. Why?"

"You're the genius."

"The other night when I followed O'Brien, they went to that warehouse off of Lake Street. It's where I found that card of the storage company."

"Who could forget."

"Hold on, the prisoner O'Brien brought, now that I think about it, was Beth Daniels. I'm sure of it."

"How sure?"

Billy Dee checked Shep's phone. "Here the picture."

"Well?"

"Hmm."

"Not sure?"

Billy Dee looked from the photo to his partner. "It was dark out there and I couldn't exactly walk up to them and ask."

"You'd be great at a lineup."

They had reached Chicago and LaSalle and traffic slowed.

"What's with all these cars?" Shep asked.

"Keep your eyes on the road, and I'll people watch."

"Sure thing. I'm reassured. I've got Davy Crockett in the passenger seat."

"No way, he wasn't African American."

"Name one of yours who was as good a sharp-shooter."

Billy Dee chomped down on his unlit cigar and after a minute said, "Ben Hodge."

"Right, you made the name up."

"No sir, Google it, you'll...hold on. That's her. I swear. She's with a tall Black guy and they're walking north. Pull over."

Chapter Eighty

Jack enjoyed this woman's sexuality. Her skin was soft and her tits supple and responsive. He grabbed her ass. Her movement sent pleasure soaring through him. Her eyes were closed, as if all she wanted was to soak up every sensation. His thrusts were met with hers. He was almost totally enveloped in this sensuality when he heard a noise and it wasn't the bedsprings. He strained to hear the sound again. He slowed, but this woman was too good. Maybe it was Ivan. He looked at this female fucking the shit out of him and grabbed her tit. His tongue went over her nipple, producing a moan. He closed his eyes for a second but then heard something again… the creak of a floor board. His eyes darted from the gyrating woman who seemed oblivious to the doorway, then back to her. She now straddled him with her arms and rocked her lower body. She began to pant.

***

Susan focused on the room at the front of the house. One step at a time, but every sound she made seemed amplified… the creak of the floor, her breathing. But her movement didn't stop the bedsprings and the moans. It seemed to take forever to get within twenty feet. She wiped the sweat from her face and inched closer. Despite the dim light, shadows of figures were on a bed. *Shit, who was who.* She hugged the wall next to the doorway with her back. *Think.* She listened. There seemed to be a pause in the moans. Then a guttural "yes, yes" and higher pitch "Oh…" The sound of exhausted springs supporting the weight above became shriller as if they had not much left. *No more time. He's probably doing it missionary.*

***

Jack's concentration alternated from the doorway to the woman who was doing her best to climax. At the moment when she tightened and her body shook, he saw a shadow fly into the room. He still had the presence of mind to raise his gun.

***

Susan charged and leapt, swinging the hammer with all her force on the head of the person on top. A loud bang and cries came from somewhere until Susan realized it was she who was screaming. Pain seared through her. She couldn't feel her left shoulder. She looked wildly around. The body beneath her did not move. Blood gushed from where she landed the blow.

"Get up." It was Jack's voice.

She looked over the person beneath her. A gun was aimed at her face.

She stumbled off the bed and landed on her ass. She moved her right hand slowly to her left side, her fingers drenched with her own blood.

Chapter Eighty-One

Shep slammed on the brakes and before he was fully stopped, Billy Dee jumped out. His knee buckled. "Damn." He limped to the sidewalk.

"What the hell?" Shep caught up with him. "This isn't *I Spy*. I'm not Robert Culp."

Billy Dee rubbed his leg and gave him a look. "Don't you think for a moment I'm Bill Cosby."

"Let me see. Nah, he's fatter than you…same cigar."

"Nice… Okay, I think they're a half a block away."

They eased their way through the crowded sidewalk with Billy Dee a step or two behind.

"Does everyone have to do their Christmas shopping all on the same day?" Shep asked. "The stores aren't giving things away."

"Get in the spirit. I think they're up ahead."

They reached the corner just as the light changed and saw the pair cross to the other side.

"Damn," Billy Dee said, "they are getting off Michigan and going west. This could work better. They won't know we're following them."

After a block and a half, they found themselves between Rush and State. Billy Dee, still slightly behind his partner, saw that Beth and the man with her stopped walking and stood beside a black SUV.

"Now's the time," Billy Dee said, "if they get into the car we're screwed."

Shep turned. "We cross and we give ourselves away."

"No choice." Billy Dee stepped into the street. "If they ask we can say we're crossing guards."

"What? In the middle of the street."

Billy Dee didn't wait. He reached the other side and took a few steps toward the couple.

"Ms. Daniels?"

She looked up and edged closer to the car door.

"Ms. Daniels, my name is Billy Dee Jackson and this is Detective Sheppard from the Chicago Police."

"Not again. I'm through with you assholes."

"Detective Sheppard is from Bomb and Arson. Your husband was a victim in that blast at the Palace Garage."

"I'm aware. So?"

"We'd like to talk to you about it."

"Well, I don't want to talk to you."

The Black man stepped closer to her. "Why you hassl'n this woman?"

"This doesn't concern you… Mr. King."

"Say what? Where you get dis King name. I didn't say noth'n."

"You're famous in these parts." Billy Dee turned to Ms. Daniels. "I understand you had a rough night with Detective O'Brien. But here's the thing, the parking lot has cameras. We're waiting for the film now. The E.T. boys found parts of the explosive device and they are checking for DNA. You get where I'm going with this?"

She looked from Billy Dee to King and hugged the file tighter. "I…eh…"

King leaned over and whispered something.

"You're what?" she screamed, "I don't fuck'n believe… Listen," she said to Billy Dee, "I've got something you may be interested. It's in this folder." She gave King a look and moved closer to the detectives.

Shep moved forward. "Be happy to take a look. Why don't you come with us."

King put a hand on Beth's shoulder. "I'll be happy to drive."

"Huh?" The two men said in unison.

King reached into his coat pocket. Billy Dee felt his pocket for his gun.

"Allow me to introduce myself. My name is John Bennett and I work for the US government, ATF. Here's my ID. We've been building a case against Beth's husband Joe Daniels for a couple of years."

"What's he done?" Billy Dee asked.

"He sells guns to the gangs and we're rolling the bangers up as we speak."

"I'll be damned," Billy Dee said. "Where does Ms. Daniels come in?"

"That file she's holding has the records of what Joe has done."

"What about the bombing at the Palace?"

Bennett looked at Beth. "What about it, Ms. Daniels? Revenge?"

Chapter Eighty-Two

Jack maneuvered himself out of the bed. He leaned over the body that had been on top of him and checked for a pulse. "You killed her," he said to Susan. "Too bad, she was very good." He stepped around and stood over Susan. "I could force you to finish what…" He nodded in the direction of the dead woman. "But the mood is gone, as you can see."

She didn't look but kept her head down and whimpered.

He grabbed her arm. She shrieked. "You need to look at me when I speak. *C'est des manieres communes.*"

"Your French stinks," she managed to say.

"Perhaps." He looked at the wall behind, then at her. "You are lucky. The bullet went through and through."

"How do you know?"

He pointed at the spot. "So that means we apply pressure to stop the bleeding." He looked around and settled on part of the sheet to rip with his hands. He then wrapped it around the wound. "I don't want you to die just yet. Hell, Ivan may have a use for you." He snickered. "And later maybe I do too."

He dressed but kept an eye on her. "You know you ruined a great fuck," he said, putting his boots on. "She, whoever she was, went all out. It's rare to find women like that. Okay, now you will get up."

Susan hesitated. "I can't. I'm dizzy. I think I'm about to faint."

He grabbed her chin. He stared into her face and weighed

his next step. "I'll help." He grasped her under her good arm and lifted. He let her lean on him as they moved to the kitchen. "Sit by that wall."

She did as she was told.

"Thirsty?"

Her yes was barely audible.

He opened several cabinets and found a glass which he filled with water.

"Drink, but slowly. I'm going to wake Ivan. I can't believe he slept through all this."

He went down the stairs and flicked on the lights. "God in heaven, what the fuck happened?" He spun around and gazed at the corners of the room. With his gun pointed, he stepped into the bathroom and shower area. There was nothing to see.

He went back to the bodies in the lower bedroom. He stooped and checked Ivan, who was on the floor. A foot or two from him was another gun. He picked it up and stuck it under his belt. He then went to the bed and looked at the dead man who was half undressed. "Who the fuck are you?"

Jack rubbed his face with his pistol hand, trying to make sense of this scene along with the dead girl upstairs. After a minute or two, he realized there was nothing more to do. Whatever happened was not for him to figure out. His mission was to get the guns for the Serbian Liberation Army.

He took the stairs two at a time and grabbed his prisoner. She dropped the glass as he pulled her up.

"Time's up," he said. "Dumond told me you know where they are."

"What? What are you talking about?"

He pushed her out the side door into the garage. "Are you stupid? Don't you know Dumond told me everything? How else would I find you? I also know about Dmursic and Hugo." He tightened his hold on her and stared into her face.

"I know you went to Hugo. Then he disappeared until the police found him in his bed, dead from a gunshot wound."

"Let go of me."

"Not on your life." He looked around the garage and saw a red can on the floor. "Move." He picked up the canister and twisted the top. He smelled the contents and said, "Good." Then he pushed her to the back of the parked van. "Put your hands on the handle." He placed his hands over hers and poured the liquid into the vehicle. The can went in too. He took out a knife from his pocket and cut material from the bottom of Susan's shirt. "Where are the guns?

Susan was bent over with her hand on the rear bumper.

"If you don't want to die tell me, otherwise…"

"Please."

"Please don't burn you? You have till three. One, two…"

"All right." Her voice cracked. Jack's hand was on the small of her back. "The guns are at a storage place."

"What's the name?"

"Allied Storage."

"Where?"

"On Clark near Addison."

"And the locker number?"

She turned to look at him. "Oh God." Jack placed more pressure on her pushing her forward. "2475D." She took a breath. "Without me, you won't get in."

"Is that so?" He paused, then grabbed what was left of her shirt and pushed her out of the way. He lit the material and tossed the flaming torch into the van. He pushed Susan out and closed the garage door. They half ran, half glided down the driveway toward his white vehicle. "Get in the back like you did before." It took a minute or two to bind her legs tight. "Be glad you're still alive."

He jumped into the driver's seat and drove away. In his mirror, he saw smoke pouring from the abandoned house.

Chapter Eighty-Three

"Hello, Mr. Daniels, this is Billy Dee Jackson, we have your wife at the station."

"You do? Did she do it? That bitch."

"We're looking into it. But when we picked her up, she had a legal file. Is it yours?"

"A file? What file?

"Not sure, but it's a brown folder with your firm's name on it."

"That bitch. She probably stole it from my office."

"Great, we'll send a car for you. You need to identify it."

"Why? I already told you it's mine."

"Mr. Daniels, you know that's not good enough."

"I'm not feeling well. I'm still suffering from the explosion."

"I understand, that's why you'll be picked up. The procedure won't take long. ID the file and you'll go home."

Daniels voice faded.

"Mr. Daniels?"

"I, eh, you know maybe it's not mine. She could have gotten it from anywhere."

"That's why you need to come down. If it's yours and she had no permission, then she committed a crime."

"Thanks, officer. I know what the law is." He paused, "Okay, I'll be down in five minutes."

"An officer will meet you at the front door."

Billy Dee hung up. "Well, he's on his way," he told Shep and Bennett. "Let's finish with Ms. Daniels."

The interview room was brightly lit at the Bomb and Arson Unit on Fillmore. Ms. Daniels had a cup of coffee in front of her. Shep plopped a stack of papers and DVD discs on the table. He picked one up and held it in front of Daniels.

"This," he said, "is the video from the parking lot." He slid it into the computer and showed the screen. "You see the time stamp? It says 3:45 p.m., November 25, 2016. Now look."

A woman dressed in a beige raincoat and holding a brief-case stepped into the elevator and punched five. She left the elevator at that floor.

Shep stopped the computer. "That's you. Isn't it."

Daniels swallowed the coffee. She held the cup in both of her hands and then placed it gently on the table. "Okay… eh…" She turned to Bennett and took a deep breath. Her voice shook. "Revenge. No. Not revenge, more like freedom. I couldn't stand it anymore. Do you know what it's like to be ignored?" She shook her head. "No, that doesn't cut it. To be not acknowledged like this cup. Use it and then toss it in the garbage. That's what it was like. I found Sonny, or maybe he found me. Whatever he did when he was away from me didn't matter. He told me I was wonderful and beautiful in every way. I didn't know anything about guns or his other life."

"How did you learn to make a bomb?" Bennett asked.

"Besides being in theatre, I took chemistry as a minor. Weird combination, but I have strange interests. Besides, you can find anything on the Internet and the library."

"Where did you put it together?"

"We have a nice size storage room in the basement of our condominium building. Few people go there, and there's plenty of room. I had a lot of spare time with Joe."

Billy Dee's mobile buzzed. He picked it up, said a few words, and then hit Off.

"Well here goes."

The officers left the interview room and locked the door. They found Mr. Daniels in another room.

Shep and Billy Dee walked in. "Evening, Mr. Daniels," Billy Dee said, "I'm glad you felt well enough."

"Not really, but get on with it. Where's the file? Has the bitch confessed?" His eyes were steady.

"I'll put it this way, Mr. Daniels, she ain't going anywhere any time soon."

He rubbed his hands together. "Great job. I was almost killed. I don't understand it, though, She, had everything. Why?" He shook his head. "Just goes to show how ungrateful a woman can be. Fifteen years."

Shep slid the closed file recovered from Ms. Daniels over to his partner. "Is this the file you say she stole?" He held it up.

"Let me put on my glasses. Yes, the Simon file. That's the one."

"Any reason why she would take that one?"

"Who knows how the bitch thinks? She probably grabbed the first one she saw off my desk."

"But Mr. Daniels, it wasn't on your desk. Was it?"

"I, eh, I don't know. My desk is a mess. Papers all over the place. It could have been. What's this about?"

Billy Dee sat back. "There's someone we'd like you to meet." He got up and opened the door.

"Mr. Daniels, this is Mr. John Bennett of the Alcohol, Tobacco, Firearms, and Explosives unit of the Federal Government. You know him by his other name… Andre King." Billy Dee saw Daniels slump in his chair. "By the way, Mr. Daniels, after what's in dat file and all of the conversations you had with this gentleman, you ain't go'in anywhere soon neither."

Chapter Eighty-Four

J ack kept his eyes on the road. Night driving was good for speed, and making up distance, but it was a struggle to stay awake. The noise of the radio blended into the sound of the tires on the road. He began to talk. "Susan," he called out, "such a beautiful girl, how did you get in involved with Dumond? He's a little old for you. No?" He glanced at the rearview mirror.

"Don't feel like talking? Not a problem. Dumond was scum."

"Is he alive?" Her voice was weak.

"Oh, so you do talk. No, *ma petite*, he met his end at a very nice restaurant/hotel. You know he loved women, and that was his doom."

"You lie."

"Whatever. Tell me, were you also fucking this Anatoly Dmursic besides Hugo?"

The wind buffeted the van, and he had to steer to the right to stay in his lane. "I didn't hear what you say. Dmursic."

"What about him?" she asked.

"Was he your lover too?"

"Sure, why not. Everyone was my lover. You can be too."

"Good to know."

"Is Dmursic still alive?"

He arched his eyebrows and bounced in his seat when the van hit a bump. "You say Dmursic. Hmm, now it makes sense. Yes. That must have been you."

"What? I didn't…what must have been me?"

"I found out that Dmursic was buying guns from Hugo. The same guns that were promised to us by your friend Dumond. Anyway, when I went to his apartment, I saw a woman leave. It must have been you."

She didn't answer.

He looked in the mirror. "That's okay, your pussy always has room for one more, and whether it's Dumond, Dmursic, or Hugo, it makes no difference to you. *C'est la vie, ma petite.*" He laughed.

The Interstate rolled into the outskirts of the city. There were now lights on the highway. He slowed to the speed limit and read the posted signs. He glanced up.

"It won't be long."

Chapter Eighty-Five

"I'm tell'n you we should go back to the storage place," Billy Dee said to Shep.

"Aren't you tired? Don't you need to sleep? Your wife…"

"Don't you worry about Janine none. I feel it. I was at Hugo's. Ain't no guns there. It has to be at the storage place. Now that I recollect, I'm damn sure it was a woman I saw in Hugo's doorway. Now she know the heat is on and she needs to get the guns out of there."

"All right. You're giving me a headache. I'm going to finish the paperwork on Beth Daniels, grab some water, and then we'll go."

Billy Dee smiled. "See'n the look on Joe Daniels' face when Bennett stepped in the room, why, he almost crapped in his pants."

Shep glanced up from the forms he was filling out and cracked a smile. "It makes do'n this job all worth it."

"It sure do."

***

The van stopped near the front of the storage company. Jack went to the truck's back door and opened it. "Sit up, and drink, but do it slow." He gave her a bottle of water, then cut the ropes around her legs. "All right, nice and easy. If you screw this up, I'll shoot you on the spot."

They walked the few steps to the entrance. He had his hand under her good shoulder to support her.

"Okay, do your magic," he said.

"I need my purse. The card is in there."

His grip tightened. She grimaced from the pain. "There will be more than that if you're fucking with me." He eased the pressure. As she turned toward the vehicle, she kicked him in the balls. Her blow made him double over, then sink to his knees. All the air went out of him. It took several seconds to recover.

"You bitch." He grabbed his gun from his pocket. The van took off. He fired.

***

"Shots fired, shots fired," Shep yelled into his radio. Billy Dee drove the car within inches of the man with the gun. The brights of the vehicle aimed at his face. Shep leapt from the car. "Police, drop the gun."

The man seemed shocked. He tried to shield his eyes, but Shep grabbed him and forced him to the ground.

Billy Dee ran up and kicked the Beretta away.

***

Susan turned the corner at Belmont and slowed down. She drove for a few more blocks, turned on a side street, and parked. Then she wiped the steering wheel with the sleeve of her shirt, left the keys in the ignition, and locked the door. She knew how to disappear.

***

It was evening in Chicago and near Christmas. Snow

fell lightly upon the roads. Despite the weather, the airport was not as crowded as Susan imagined. The security line moved fast and she breezed through. This time her passport had her real name- Simone Dubois. The departure board displayed her flight. It was Gate K1. She took her time to walk to the boarding area. She sighed… She had learned more than she ever wanted to about Chicago. The weeks it took her to recover. The moving from one flea-bitten hotel to another—all the aliases, disguises, and lies. Dumond had taught her well. It was time to go home.